Amos Andrew Parker

Recollections of General Lafayette on his Visit to the United States

In 1824 and 1825 with the Most Remarkable Incidents of his Life...

Amos Andrew Parker

Recollections of General Lafayette on his Visit to the United States
In 1824 and 1825 with the Most Remarkable Incidents of his Life...

ISBN/EAN: 9783337058289

Printed in Europe, USA, Canada, Australia, Japan

Cover: Foto ©Raphael Reischuk / pixelio.de

More available books at **www.hansebooks.com**

RECOLLECTIONS

OF

GENERAL LAFAYETTE

ON HIS

VISIT TO THE UNITED STATES,

IN 1824 AND 1825;

WITH THE

MOST REMARKABLE INCIDENTS OF HIS LIFE,

FROM HIS BIRTH TO THE DAY OF HIS DEATH.

By A. A. PARKER, Esq.,

AUTHOR OF "TRIP TO THE WEST AND TEXAS;" "POEMS AT
FOURSCORE," &C.

"Though lost to sight, to memory dear."

KEENE, N. H.:
SENTINEL PRINTING COMPANY, BOOK AND JOB PRINTERS.
1879.

INTRODUCTORY.

My Recollections of General Lafayette's visit to this country in 1824 and '25, were narrated in the State House at Concord, N. H., at the request of the Historical Society. It was merely an extemporary affair, as I had nothing then written before me. I was requested to write out, at my leisure, my Recollections for publication, with such emendations and additions as the subject seemed to require. This, I have done; and the result will be found in the following pages. I have corresponded extensively and searched records, so as to give a connected Sketch of his eventful life, from his birth to the day of his death.

My object has been to snatch from oblivion and garner up the most remarkable events in the life of a most remarkable man, so that the present generation may be well informed of the true character of one of our most patriotic Major Generals in the American Revolution. Much interesting matter is here presented, never before published; a large portion of which was obtained from the General himself. On his visit here, it was my good fortune to become acquainted with him, and learn from his own lips, his opinion of men and things, and many remarkable incidents in his life. I was then, as now, a great admirer of his character; for I deem him to have been one of the most brave, active and faultless men, of whom we have any account in ancient or modern history.

The preparation of this Sketch, has been a labor of love; and while I have entered into the spirit of the times, I have endeavored to be entirely correct; and believe its integrity cannot successfully be impeached; but that in all its essential particulars, it will stand the test of talents and of time.

In this Sketch, I have uniformly applied the title of GENERAL, to Lafayette, as he publicly renounced that of *Marquis*, at the time of the French revolution.

————

In the Frontispiece will be found a steel engraving of General Lafayette. It was taken from a portrait painting of him in 1824, at the age of 67. It is a most perfect likeness. At the bottom is his autograph.

CONTENTS.

RECOLLECTIONS OF GEN. LAFAYETTE,

AND SKETCH OF HIS LIFE.

The great English poet asks, What's in a NAME? I answer, MUCH. · Names are often, not only music to the ear, but expressive of power, and suggestive of noble men and glorious deeds. And when I announce LAFAYETTE, as the theme of my discourse, is it not suggestive of a Statesman, Patriot and Warrior, who most nobly wielded his sword and pen, and gave of his substance liberally, in the cause of human rights, and bravely fought the battles of our Revolution?

Permit me then, standing on the verge of time, between the living and the dead, to call your attention to one of the most exciting scenes in the annals of our history since the days of our revolution. In 1824, more than half a century ago, The MARQUIS GILBERT MOTIER DE LAFAYETTE, for the *Fourth Time*, visited the United States. His arrival was hailed with universal joy throughout the land; and he passed through the twenty-four States of the Union, in a round of civic and martial triumphs, unequalled in magnificence and splendor. During that visit, it was my good fortune to become acquainted with him, and to witness some of the most splendid displays on that occasion; and I propose now to relate my recollections of what I saw and heard, in the order of

2

events, rather than in the order I obtained knowledge of them. If the narration should be deemed too much bordering on the sentimental, and withal, too egotistical, I cannot avoid it, without mystifying events and perverting facts. Enthusiastic I must be, for my subject demands it. But in the first place, allusion to his former visits may be interesting and proper as introductory to the last.

The *First Time* Gen. Lafayette visited this country was in 1777, about a year after the Declaration of Independence. When his intention of aiding the Colonies in their struggle for independence was suspected, or, to some extent known, it caused a great sensation both in England and France. The British Minister at Paris so warmly protested against it that the King of France was induced to issue an order for his arrest; but he had the sagacity to elude all pursuit, ordered his vessel to an obscure port in Spain, where he embarked, and from thence sailed for the American coast.

When he fitted out his own ship, freighted with arms and munitions of war, it was the most gloomy time in the revolutionary war. The British armies were everywhere triumphant, so much so, that even the firmness of Gen. Washington was shaken. Lafayette's friends urged him to desist from such a hopeless undertaking, but he gallantly replied that it was the very time his aid was most needed.

After a devious and tedious voyage of more than two months, for he had to avoid the numerous British cruisers on the American coast, on the 14th of June, 1777, he landed at Winyau Bay, on the South Carolina coast, 60 miles Northeast of Charleston. He was accompanied by his friend, the Baron de Kalb, a German officer of rank; and when their boat touched the shore at midnight, they both pledged themselves before high Heaven, to win Independence or perish in the attempt. And they most nobly redeemed their pledge; for they both most bravely fought the battles of the Revolution. Gen. Lafayette passed through all the severe conflicts with only a flesh wound, but the Baron was less fortunate, for, after three years of hard fighting, he was killed at the battle of Camden, in North Carolina, August 16, 1780, and was taken from the field with eleven wounds on his body.

They were, at first, very hospitably entertained at the mansion house of Maj. Benjamin Huger, and then proceeded to Charleston. They procured a carriage and started for Philadelphia together. Their route lay through the principal towns, yet the roads were so bad that the carriage soon became a wreck, and they finished their journey on horseback.

General Lafayette's arrival, at that critical moment, caused no ordinary sensation throughout the country. It was hailed as a happy omen, and gave a new impulse to the revolutionary struggle.

Although he was then a mere youth, hardly twenty years of age; yet, so active and patriotic was he, that Congress, on the 31st of July, 1777, appointed him a Major-General in the Continental Army. As there was no vacancy at the time, no particular command could be assigned him; but he was invited to the headquarters of Gen. Washington, and became an inmate of his family, and acted as his aid, companion and friend during the war, when not assigned to a separate command.

On the 11th of September, less than a month and a half after his appointment, was fought the battle of Brandywine; and then, his shrewdness, activity and bravery fully justified his appointment; for it was readily perceived that he had, in an eminent degree, the three essential attributes of a successful warrior; for he was quick to perceive, sagacious to plan, and prompt to execute. In that battle he was wounded, and had to be confined for a time in a hospital; but it was the only time he was disabled from active duty during the perils of the Revolution.

On the 11th day of February, 1779, he returned to France to obtain men, money and munitions of war. Being successful in that, he returned here a *Second Time,* on the 27th of April, 1780, and rendered very efficient aid in many battles and skirmishes, until the surrender of Lord Cornwallis, at Yorktown, on the 19th of October, 1781.

Deeming the back of British power in America broken, and that a bold dash would finish it, on the 22d of December, 1781, he again returned to France for an army of men and ships of war. He induced the King of Spain as well as of France, to second his wishes; and, in time, had obtained 60 ships of war and enlisted 24,000 men, which began to assemble at Cadiz, destined to crush British power in America as well as in the West Indies.

Then the King of England and his ministers took the alarm, began to realize their danger, and acknowledged our independence and concluded a peace. On the 20th day of January, 1783, the treaty of peace was finally concluded and signed at Paris.

General Lafayette was then at Cadiz, preparing to sail for America and bring the joyful news of peace; but finding some diplomatic difficulties in Spain which he was requested to adjust, and seeing the need of a commercial treaty between the United States and France, in which he believed his services were needed, he deemed it his duty to remain. But he procured a fast sailing ship of war, called the Triumph, (an appropriate name for the occasion,) and sent the despatches, with a letter to Congress and to General Washington, bearing the joyful tidings of peace. The Triumph arrived at Philadelphia on the 23d day of March, 1783, and gave to Congress and the Nation the first news of peace.

Congress passed strong resolutions in commendation of

the great services of General Lafayette; and Washington, in a letter to him, said: "To this cause, (alluding to the armament of Lafayette), I am persuaded the peace is to be ascribed."

Although Gen. Lafayette was earnestly and most cordially invited to visit this country, by Congress and Gen. Washington, he forebore the pleasure until he had settled other matters of more pressing importance. He went to Spain and settled the difficulties there, and then returned to Paris, and was the leading spirit in forming a commercial treaty between the two countries. This was a work of time, involving so many conflicting interests, that it was not fully completed in all its details for more than a year.

On his *Third Visit* to America, he came in the royal frigate La Nymphe, and landed at New York city on the 4th day of August, 1784. It so happened, that in the whole of the Revolution, he had never been in the city of New York; and its citizens, as if to make up for lost time, gave him a most splendid reception. Among the many great attentions shown him, was a grand entertainment the next day after his arrival, at which his comrades in arms appeared in uniform in honor of the occasion.

He entered the city of Philadelphia with the shouts of the multitude, ringing of bells and firing of cannon. Generals Wayne, Irwin and St. Clair were deputed to congratulate him on his arrival and welcome him to the city. The Legislature of Pennsylvania, then in session, voted him a flattering address, and the citizens at large vied with each other to do him honor.

On the 14th of August, he left Philadelphia, staid a short time in Baltimore, and arrived at Mount Vernon, the seat of General Washington, on the 19th. An account of this interview between such long-tried and cordial friends, that I may not be accused of bordering too much on the sentimental, I give in the eloquent words of another : " When we reflect upon the principal events in the lives of these two illustrious men—the difference in their ages and countries—the distance which separated them from each other—the circumstances which brought them together—the importance of the scenes through which they had passed—the glorious success of their courageous efforts—their mutual anxiety again to embrace each other—the tender and truly paternal esteem of the one, and the respect, admiration and filial attachment of the other—when we reflect upon all this, we find that everything contributed to stamp this interesting interview with a sublimity of character which had no prototype in the annals of men."

Twelve blissful days were spent at Mount Vernon, and then he went to the North, and aided in the negotiations with the Indians at Fort Schuyler. The Indians believed in " Kayewla," as they called Lafayette, took his advice and made peace with the whites. After making presents to the Chiefs, he left them, with a treaty fully ratified, and proceeded, through Albany, Hartford and Worcester, to Boston. Enthusastic demonstrations awaited him all along the route; but it was at Boston that he had the most splendid triumph. A magnificent military procession, bearing the flags of America and France, with a vast multitude of citizens, escorted him into the metropolis, and through the principal streets, amid the ringing of bells, firing of cannon, and shouts of the multitude. Illuminations in his honor and fireworks on the Common were the order of the night.

On the 19th of October, the anniversary of the surrender of Lord Cornwallis, a grand dinner was given at the City Hotel. A grand procession was formed, composed of the Governor, Council and members of the Legislature, accompanied by the old continental officers, soldiers

and citizens, under escort of military companies, and
proceeded to the great saloon of the Hotel, where entertainment had been provided for five hundred persons.
Thirteen arcades were thrown across the Hall, emblemati-
cal of the thirteen States of the Union. Lafayette was
seated beneath the centre arch, where a wreath of flowers
was suspended. After dinner thirteen toasts were drank,
and each one was enthusiastically cheered by the band of
music and thirteen guns in State Street. When the health
of Washington was announced as the last toast, a curtain
immediately fell and disclosed a portrait of him, encircled
by laurels and decorated with the flags of America and
France. Lafayette arose and gazed at it with a look of
pleasure and surprise, when a voice exclaimed, "Long
live Washington !" The effect was electrical—all arose
as one man—shouts of "Long live Washington" resounded throughout the Hall, and in that enthusiastic
manner the feast ended.

From Boston, he visited the towns of Salem, Marblehead, Gloucester, Beverley, Ipswich, Newburyport and
Portsmouth, N. H. Returning to Boston, he embarked
again in the La Nymphe, which had come round from
New York, and sailed away to the theatre of his greatest
glory, the Chesapeake Bay. He landed at Yorktown, and
it was with no ordinary emotions he viewed the scenes
of one of the greatest struggles for American independence. It was in Virginia that he had baffled the manœu-
vres of one of the most accomplished and bravest Generals of Europe, and finally compelled him to surrender
with his whole army and munitions of war.

From Yorktown, he proceeded to Williamsburg, where
he received a most cordial reception, and on the 18th of
November entered the city of Richmond ; and here he
met with a reception transcending, if possible, all former
displays. Gen. Washington was in waiting for him here,

and after receiving the enthusiastic congratulations of the Legislature and citizens, he accompanied, once more, his venerable and revered friend to the shades of Mount Vernon. After staying there about a week, and visiting Alexandria, they proceeded to Annapolis, and here, they took an affectionate leave of each other. Gen. Washington, not satisfied with this one leave-taking, on his return home, wrote him a farewell letter, bordering more on the sentimental than any other of his numerous correspondence. They never met again, but corresponded with each other until the death of Washington, in 1799.

Journeying Northward, he took leave of Congress, then in session at Trenton. Mr. Jay, as Chairman of a Congressional Committee, presented the resolutions of that body, with an impassioned address of his own; to which, Gen. Lafayette exclaimed: "May this immense temple of freedom ever stand, a lesson to the oppressed, and a sanctuary for the rights of mankind." Patriotism now, with a voice that seems to wake the dead, utters the same invocation throughout our wide and extended domain, and rejoices that it has withstood the shock of one of the most gigantic rebellions ever known among men.

On the 25th of December, 1784, he embarked at New York, on board the La Nymphe, which had come round to that port to receive him, sailed for France, and arrived in Paris on the 25th of January, 1785.

In 1824, just forty years after he had taken his leave of Washington, he paid his *Fourth*, and *Last Visit*, to this country. When he signified his intention of visiting his American friends, President Munroe, authorized by Congress, tendered him a national ship. This, he declined, alleging that, as he came in no official capacity, but as a private citizen, he preferred to embark in a merchant packet ship.

When his intention of visiting this country was known

in France, it became manifest to him that the king, Louis
XVIII., was opposed to the movement, and would prevent it if he could find any plausible pretext for so doing.
For the king was well aware that his visit would occasion
many public patriotic speeches, which would be reported,
and published in France, and cause discontent among the
people, and perhaps, danger to the throne itself. Therefore, it was, when he arrived at Havre, and made preparations to embark, he was beset by a large police force,
who harrassed his steps: and when anyone made any
demonstration of joy at his presence, he was at once arrested and imprisoned. He felt that he was watched, and
had he made any address to the crowd, would have been
arrested and prevented from visiting this country at all.
He, therefore, said not a word, but waved his hand to
the people and quietly embarked.

It was in the American packet ship, Cadmus, Capt.
Allyn, that he embarked; and after a pleasant voyage of
thirty-one days, he arrived at the port of New York, on
the 14th day of August, 1824. It was Sunday, and by
invitation of Vice-President Thompkins, he landed at
Staten Island and spent the Sabbath with him.

On Monday morning, he arose early and walked out to
exercise his limbs on shore. It was a beautiful day. The
sun rose bright and clear in the East. On turning to
look in the opposite direction, he beheld a beautiful, high
arched rainbow over the land in the West. He hailed it
as a happy omen, and deemed it to be a bow of welcome
as well as of promise. But when he saw the fleet of
steamers coming to escort him to the city of New York,
he was amazed at what he beheld. There was a squadron
of eight steamers—the Chancellor Livingston, Bellona,
Connecticut, Oliver Ellsworth, Henry Eckford, Nautilus,
Olive Branch, and the steam frigate Robert Fulton—all
gaily dressed for the occasion; with bands of music, flags

3

flying, and filled with joyous ladies and gentlemen. On reaching the shore, the Fulton gave a national salute, flags waved as well as ladies' white handkerchiefs, the bands of music saluted and the men shouted a welcome. The General was shouted aboard the steamer Chancellor Livingston; two others grappled the ship Cadmus, took it in tow, and then all turned their prows to the city of New York, some ten miles away. It was a most beautiful day, and when this flotilla of steamers started, led by the Chancellor Livingston, salutes, shouts and cheers awakened the echoes along the shore, and the big guns of Brooklyn uttered their deep toned voices across the water, and made the steamers tremble as they passed.

On landing at the Battery, he was met by a multitude that no man could number, introduced to many citizens, partook of some refreshment at Castle Garden, and then took a seat with Gen. Morton in an open barouche and proceeded up Broadway to be introduced to the Mayor at the City Hall. As he proceeded, he cast a look above and around him, and such a gorgeous display he had seldom or never witnessed, even in excitable France. He there beheld triumphal arches, flags suspended across the street, joyous men, women and children, on house tops, balconies, and in windows, on sidewalks and in the streets; bands of music playing, bells ringing, men shouting and women waving their handkerchiefs; and then flowers, in bouquets and wreaths, came showering down from all quarters, so that the horses at times literally "walked on flowers;" made such a display, in extent so unexpected, and in such contrast to the manner of his leaving France, that he was completely overwhelmed; and, on reaching City Hall, had to step aside into an ante-room to wipe away his tears, and compose himself before entering the audience hall.

As he had promised a flying visit to Boston to see his

revolutionary friends, before paying his respects to the General Government at Washington, he stayed only four days in the city of New York. Supposing he was to furnish his own conveyance to Boston, he sent his servant to procure the needful equipage. The servant soon returned and announced that the carriages would be at the door in less than an hour. When the carriages came, an officer, with an escort, came with them. When he was about to step on board, he inquired of the officer when, where and how much he was to pay for his conveyance to Boston. The officer turned and said, "General Lafayette! you are the NATION'S GUEST; you can pay nothing while you remain in America—all your wants will be abundantly supplied by a grateful people, without money and without price."

And he found the announcement of the officer literally true, for he had not been permitted to expend a dollar on his whole trip throughout the States of the Union.

He found himself seated in an elegant carriage with a splendid escort, and on his way to Boston. On coming to a toll gate, he observed two men in a carriage before him, who had stopped to pay toll. The toll gate was open, the keeper came to the door of the toll house, waved his hand, and said: "Go ahead! the road is free; General Lafayette travels this road to-day, and no man pays toll."

He left New York on the 20th of August, and was four days on his trip through Connecticut and Rhode Island to Boston. He had a splendid escort all the way, and great demonstrations of joy were made by the citizens of the several towns and villages through which he passed. He took the lower route near the sea coast, through Bridgeport, New Haven, New London and Providence, R. I. He was so much delayed by the demonstrations on the way, that he had to travel sometimes in the night.

It was midnight when he entered Dedham, yet he found the village illuminated and the people all wide awake to give him a cordial reception. Late at night, or rather early in the morning, he arrived at the mansion house of Gov. Eustis, in Roxbury. The meeting between these revolutionary friends was most cordial; they did, indeed, "cry for joy."

On Tuesday, Aug. 24, a large cavalcade, and citizens in carriages and on foot, escorted him to Boston. The procession passed through the principal streets, amid the ringing of bells, firing of cannon and shouts of the multitude. On the East side of the Common, three thousand school children of both sexes, dressed in uniform, with ribbons on the breast stamped with likenesses of Lafayette, were paraded in two lines; they saluted the General as he passed, and their shrill voices were distinctly heard above the din of the hour. The General's carriage paused for a moment while he turned to salute the children, when a Miss of some ten summers darted from the line, leaped into his carriage and placed a wreath of laurel, interwoven with flowers, on his head. He impressed a kiss on her blushing cheek as she retired. Immediately he placed the wreath on the seat beside him, and found a neatly folded paper attached, containing the following lines, which he read at his leisure :—

> "An infant hand presents these blushing flowers,
> Glowing and pure as childhood's artless hours:
> Twined with the laurel Fame on thee bestowed,
> When thy young heart with patriot ardor glowed.
> Self-exiled from the charms of wealth and love,
> And home, and friends, thou did'st our champion prove;
> And by the side of glorious Washington,
> Did'st make our grateful country all thine own.
> Go, fragile offering, speak the ardent joy
> Our bosoms feel, which time can ne'er destroy."

Beautiful arches were thrown across many of the principal streets, covered with evergreens and flowers. One

on Washington street was superb, and contained the following lines :—

"WELCOME, LAFAYETTE!"

"Our fathers in glory now sleep,
Who gathered with thee to the fight;
But the sons will eternally keep
The tablet of gratitude bright.

We bow not the neck,
We bend not the knee;
But our hearts, LAFAYETTE,
We surrender to thee."

As the procession came on to Beacon street, it reminded
the General of his dear revolutionary friend, Mrs. Hancock ; and he inquired of the Mayor if she was yet alive.
He was assured that she was not only alive, but of quite
good health for a person of her advanced age. And then,
says the Mayor, you will see her at the window as we
pass, and as the sashes are out, you will have a fine view
of her. As the carriage came opposite her house, the
venerable lady was seen at an open window. General
Lafayette arose in his carriage, waved his hat, hand, and
bowed to the venerable lady, while she waved her hand-
kerchief, hand, and courtesied to him. This pantomime,
between two such conspicuous characters, attracted the
attention of the crowd, and wound up with loud shouts
of applause.

General Lafayette was left by his escort at the steps of
the State House, and proceeded to the Senate Chamber,
where were assembled the Governor and Council, Judges
of Courts and revolutionary worthies. Ex-Gov. John
Brooks was present, and was recognized at once by the
General, and they had a cordial meeting. Here he was
welcomed, in behalf of the State, by Gov. Eustis ; and,
anticipating what might happen, had prepared his address
in writing. He broke down before he had completed the
first sentence, and handed it to his aid to read.

The General was then escorted to his headquarters, at the head of Park street. It is a large brick building, built for a club house, and is still standing. It was hired and fitted up by the City of Boston, as a first-class hotel, for the General's particular use and headquarters while in Boston. Being on the corner of Park and Beacon streets, and facing the Common, it is more airy and pleasant than any hotel in the city. Standing but a short distance from the State House on the East, and the Gov. Hancock house about the same distance on the West, he found time to pay a number of visits to the venerable lady Hancock. During the Revolution, and in the lifetime of her husband, he had made her house his home while in Boston. She had always treated him with all the kind attentions of an affectionate mother, and he had always esteemed her as one of his most valued friends.

In 1824, I had the pleasure of seeing the venerable lady Hancock, and looking over the ancient Hancock mansion. It stood on high ground, facing the Common, was said to have been the handsomest house in Boston when built, and then displayed many traits of architectural beauty. But where is it now? Gone! Stern modern improvement got hold of that and tore it to atoms! But the plain, staid, homely "Old South" still remains; and at a cost and on conditions that will stagger the belief of posterity. Verily, there is no accounting for taste.*

The General was escorted to Cambridge, where he attended the commencement of Harvard College, and was

---

* NOTE—It is a marvel that some of the wise antiquarians of Boston had not suggested the propriety of preserving intact the muddy shores of the frog pond on the Common, in its primitive ugliness, rather than permit it to be modernized with a neat curb-stone wall and a pleasant gravelled walk. It was the most ancient, as well as the most ugly, of anything in Boston, not excepting the "Old South." Good taste does not incline to preserve anything useless and ugly, however ancient it may be.

welcomed to that institution by the learned President Kirkland. On the Thursday following, he attended the anniversary of the *Phi Beta Kappa* Society, and listened to the impassioned eloquence of Prof. Edward Everett.

But I cannot relate all his visits, receptions and dinners during the week, in detail; and, therefore, shall only state that he went to Medford and dined with his venerable friend Gov. Brooks: and to Quincy, and spent the day with President John Adams.

And now I come to the climax of his visit at Boston, and to the first time I had the pleasure of seeing Gen. Lafayette. In 1824 and '25 I lived in Concord, N. H., was editor of a newspaper, and was an aid to Gov. Morrill,—the only time, as far as I know, when an aid of the Governor was of any importance to him, the State, or to himself. Soon after Gen. Lafayette's arrival in Boston, I received an order from the Governor to invite him to visit New Hampshire. It was at the club house where I first saw him, and although he was surrounded by many venerable men, strangers to me, yet at once I designated Lafayette from all others. I was accompanied by Gov. Eustis' aid, who called the Governor's attention to myself, and he introduced me to Gen. Lafayette. In the most fitting words I could command, in behalf of Gov. Morrill, I invited him to visit New Hampshire at his earliest convenience. He replied, that his intention was to visit New Hampshire, but not then. It had been arranged that he should be present and assist in laying the corner stone of the Bunker Hill Monument the next year, on the 17th of June, and immediately thereafter, he should be happy to pay his respects to the government and people of New Hampshire; and as the Legislature would then be in session, he deemed it to be a favorable time for his visit. I bowed assent, and he retired. The Governor stopped a moment and said: "This is the morning of a great day in Boston. Many companies of our militia will pass in review before Gen. Lafayette in front of the State House, and a great dinner will be given in a tent on the Common; and here is a ticket for the dinner. The General will also attend the Theatre at night, which will be filled to overflowing; but as I have a few reserved seats at my command, I will give you a ticket for the Theatre also. And now, if you will make yourself at home with my aid, he will give you a favorable position to witness the important coming events." And he did.

Monday, the 30th day of August, 1824, was the great display on Boston Common. Nearly 9000 troops lined the Common, the head resting on Park street gate. At ten o'clock the show began. Gen. Lafayette, accompanied by Gov. Eustis, his aids, council and many citizens, were escorted down from the State House to the Common, and formed a line on the high ground at the front. Gen. Lafayette moved a few paces in front and uncovered his head. At that moment, the commanding officer announced in a loud voice, GENERAL LAFAYETTE! The troops were standing "at ease," with ordered arms; and when this announcement was made they clapped their hands along the whole line; but as sound comes to the ear according to distance, it seemed like the prolonged roll of a drum; and then, with uncovered heads, they tried their voices in loud, rousing cheers. Whether the crowd joined in this, I know not, but I must confess I never heard such rousing cheers before. The order was then given to shoulder and present arms. Then the large band of music at the head of the column gave their thrilling cheers in three times three. In the meantime the General waved his hat and hand in recognition of these demonstrations of joy at his presence. The troops then wheeled by platoons and marched. As they passed before the General, it was manifest that enthusiasm conquered discipline.

The best drilled troops, and they were of the first order, continually broke ranks, in spite of all commands and efforts of officers. The General would occasionally smile, for he deemed the temporary disorder not a lack of discipline, but really as complimentary to himself. But sometimes the officer himself lost all thought of his men, gave the salute, faced round, advanced backwards, gazed at the General, and when his advancing men obstructed his view, turned and passed on. If the revolution tried men's souls, it would seem that Lafayette tried men's hearts.

As the General stood there in bold relief to a countless multitude—the "observed of all observers,"—I could not but notice the simplicity of his dress. The hero of two hemispheres stood there in Nankin pants, swans-down vest, blue broadcloth coat with gilt buttons, and a common beaver hat, and plain shoes on his feet,—without any insignia of rank or office on his person. What a commentary on dress now!

After the review was passed, the troops performed some well executed evolutions, and for the time were dismissed.

The public dinner was under a large tent on the high ground near the center of the Common. It was the largest and most enthusiastic feast I ever attended. There were six tables 170 feet long, with a cross table on an elevated platform at the head, on which were placed 1600 plates, and all filled. At the cross table, sat the Governor and staff, Gen. Lafayette, and a few invited guests. There were toasts prepared, and a toast-master, but the enthusiasm was so great that a rule had been made that no one should make a speech or give a volunteer toast, except through the toast-master — to be read at his discretion. But if men could not make speeches, or give toasts, it must not be supposed that it was a silent feast. They were not prohibited from talking or cheering; and when

4

the regular toasts were given, they were cheered to the
echo, more especially those that in any manner alluded to
Gen. Lafayette. The General quietly ate his dinner,
took his glass of wine, leaned back in his chair and listened awhile to the toasts, and then he and the Governor
retired. No partiality was shown, for the General was
most enthusiastically cheered in his going as well as in his
coming. I left most of the guests at the table, and how
the feast ended I know not, and never inquired.

At night, I attended the theatre, and entered a box
that my ticket indicated near the centre. The house was well
filled, and soon crowded to its utmost capacity from pit to
gallery. The play began; but no one paid any attention
to it, for all were absorbed in the expected General, and
could not attend to anything else; and he was late, for he
had to show himself at a levee and a ball, previous to his
coming there; to be introduced, more especially, to the
ladies. At length, the General, Governor and suite entered the house. The audience rose at once, and gave
such rounds of cheers as never echoed within its walls
before. It was not quite as powerful as a Southern or
Western whirlwind, for the high-arched roof held on. In
the meantime, the ladies waved their white handkerchiefs,
and the orchestra gave a salute, and then played a national
air. And then the curtain arose and showed at the back
of the stage a picture of a large castle, with the word
"LA GRANGE" at the bottom, in large letters. The General arose, waved his hat and bowed his head, in token of
recognition of his beautiful residence in France. He
afterwards told me, it was a very perfect likeness, and
must have been painted from the building itself. And
then, an actor appeared and sang a patriotic song of welcome, which was abundantly cheered and encored.

But why attempt to describe what is indescribable?
The play itself was nowhere. The actors, indeed, had

"their exits and their entrances," but no one paid any attention to them. I did not know at the time, what the play was, who the actors were, or what they said; and presume no one else did. The General totally eclipsed everything else, and at an early hour the green curtain came down and the show was over. The General was shouted aboard his carriage, and cheered along the illuminated streets; but the sound at length died away in the distance, and Boston, for a time, was at rest.

The General did not intend to extend his visit at that time, any further East than Boston, and had made his arrangements to start for New York City on the 2d day of September, at 2 o'clock P. M. But the pressure was so great, and the curiosity to see him so intense, that, through the good offices of the efficient Mayor of Boston, he consented to make a flying visit as far as Portsmouth, N. H., on the condition that he could be returned in time to fulfill his engagements.

Accordingly, he left Boston at an early hour on the 31st of August, took breakfast at Marblehead and dined at Salem at 2 P. M., staid at Newburyport over night, and appeared at Portsmouth at 8 o'clock, September 1. His visit at Portsmouth was a splendid affair, exceeding anything ever known or attempted there; before or since: an account of which fills three and a half columns of the Portsmouth Journal of that time. Only an allusion can be made to it now.

He was met at the line of Greenland by a procession, two miles long, of citizens in carriages and on horseback, and escorted to Portsmouth. On reaching Wibirds' Hill a national salute was fired by a detachment of the Portsmouth Artillery. At that point, the Strafford Guards from Dover, the Rockingham Guards and Gilman Blues joined the procession and performed escort duty through the streets of Portsmouth. On entering the compact part of the town, cannon were fired, bells rung, the men shouted a welcome and the ladies flourished their white handkerchiefs. And here, more than a thousand school children lined the street, dressed in uniform, with Lafayette badges on the breast; and their infant voices so vigorously shouted a welcome, that their shrill voices could be heard, as at Boston, above the deep-toned voices of men, martial music or the ringing of bells. After passing through Middle, Broad, Court and Congress streets, he was landed at Franklin Hall, where he was introduced to revolutionary veterans and many citizens. A grand dinner was given in Jefferson Hall, where more than three hundred young ladies were individually introduced to him. The Hall and principal buildings in Portsmouth were illuminated, and made a most splendid appearance.

He left the Hall at 10, repaired to the Gov. Langdon Mansion House, where he made his headquarters while in Portsmouth, partook of some refreshment, and at 11 was on his way, under escort, to Boston. Although he had to travel 60 miles, he was in Boston at 7 o'clock the next morning, in good time to perform all his previous engagements. He had entered Boston on the 24th of August, and left for New York on the 2d day of of September. His visit at the East was, therefore, only eight days. What a vigorous man he must have been to go through such a round of receptions, dinners and speeches, and travel so many miles in so short a time!

General Lafayette, after rest and refreshment, left Boston at 2 o'clock, passed through Lexington and Concord, stopped over night at the home of Col. Wilder at Stowe, who had been well acquainted with the General and his family in France. He then passed through Lancaster, Boston, Sterling and West Boylston to Worcester. Here he was welcomed by a large assemblage of citizens, and escorted through the principal streets. The children of

the schools were out in large numbers, ornamented with
badges of Lafayette, and threw laurels in his path as he
passed. He was here introduced to a large number of
revolutionary officers and soldiers, and the meeting was
very affecting to them both. He then passed on to Hartford in Connecticut, where his stay was short, but highly
gratifying and enthusiastic. Indeed, for the whole distance from Boston to Hartford, he had been conducted by
a continual escort and welcomed with great joy by vast
multitudes as he passed.

At Hartford, he took a steamer, called at Middletown,
and then passed down the river into Long Island Sound,
and was greatly saluted and cheered as he entered again
the City of New York.

But to be more explicit, he returned from his Eastern
tour in the steamer Oliver Ellsworth, Sept. 5, at one
o'clock P. M. A national salute was fired by the Franklin 74 as he passed; and the wharves and shores on East
River for two miles were lined with a great multitude of
citizens, who shouted continued welcomes along the whole
distance. He was received at the Fulton street wharf,
and conducted to his lodgings at the City Hotel, through
streets filled with people, whose anxiety to see him had in
no wise abated.

On the 6th of September, the anniversary of the General's birthday, for he was then 67 years old, the Cincinnati Veterans gave him a birthday dinner in Washington
Hall; and he was escorted there by the Lafayette Guards.
The room was splendidly decorated for the occasion, and
over the chair where the General sat was a triumphal arch
of evergreens and laurels, on the centre of which was a
large eagle with a scroll in his beak bearing the words
Sept. 6, 1757, the day of his birth; on the right with
a scroll bearing the words " *Brandywine, Sept. 11,*
1777," and another on the left, with the words " *York-*

town, Oct. 19, 1781." But the decorations of this Hall were so numerous and splendid, they cannot well be described in detail. Col. Varick, the president of the Society, presided, the guests were venerable and numerous, and most of them his comrades in arms during the revolution. It was to the General the most interesting banquet he had attended in America.

On Tuesday, he visited Columbia College ; and Wednesday he embarked on board the Chancellor Livingston, visited the most interesting places in the Bay, and wound up the trip at the Narrows, when a national salute was fired at Fort Lafayette. He inspected the fort, equipments and soldiers, and the visit was finished by a most delightful repast.

But time would fail me to enumerate all the honors paid the General at New York. But one was so unique and marvellous that it must not be omitted. On Thursday the fire department of New York City and Brooklyn turned out in its full strength and paraded in the Park. The fire engines numbered 46, besides a number of hook and ladder companies. The General appeared on the balcony of a hall near by, in company with a number of gentlemen and ladies, to witness the scene. In the centre of the Park, the ladders of the companies were erected in the form of a pyramid, on the top of which was placed a miniature house filled with combustibles. The engines, charged with water, then approached on all sides at a suitable distance ; at a signal the house was fired, and when in full blaze, 46 engines, from all sides, played upon it. In a twinkling, the house and fire were nowhere, but 46 streams of water from as many powerful engines, accurately directed to a common centre, shot the water high in the air like a mighty fountain, and then the spray, like silver rain, came down on all sides ; and as the sun shone, rainbows appeared in all their brilliant colors. The scene was so enchanting, unique and unexpected, that the General, as well as the ladies, could not suppress their demonstrations of joy.

On Tuesday evening, August 15, 1824, at the City Hotel, Gen. Lafayette took an affectionate leave of Capt. Allyn, of the ship Cadmus, and presented him with a superb writing desk. He also presented Daniel Chadwick, chief mate, a beautiful case of mathematical instruments, surmounted with silver; and to all the other officers and crew he gave a valued keepsake. The next day the ship Cadmus sailed for France.

But a climax of the displays at New York was reached at last, in a brilliant ball, given at Castle Garden. More than six thousand ladies and gentlemen attended; and it was, probably, the most costly and splendid ball ever given in the United States. I must leave it undescribed, for it baffles the power of speech or pen. Those that are curious in such affairs, will find an attempted description in the newspapers of the time. It must be admitted, that in extent and variety, the citizens of New York bore the palm in doing honor to Gen. Lafayette. They had the means and the will, and to these was added consummate skill.

Immediately after the ball, and at the early hour of two o'clock on Wednesday morning, the General, his son and suite, together with a large company of ladies and gentlemen, went on board the steamer James Kent, and proceeded up the river to visit Albany, the seat of government, and the intermediate towns on the route. It was a most delightful trip, not only in romantic natural scenery, but in artificial displays, at all the principal towns on the river. In addition to all this, the river banks were, generally, lined by a joyous multitude of people; and shouts of welcome echoed from shore to shore all the way to the end of the route. I cannot stop now to describe the many

enchanting scenes of the trip, as it would be too voluminous for the present occasion.

The boat returned to New York early on Sunday morning, and the General repaired to his lodgings at the City
Hotel. On Monday he dined with the Grand Lodge of
the State. Six hundred of the craft were present, decorated with all the Masonic symbols.

He then received a most interesting address from the
children of the village of Catskill, enclosing one hundred
and fifty dollars to constitute him a life member of the
American Bible Society. The General was much moved
at this, and returned a most affectionate reply.

On Thursday morning the General took a formal and
an affecting leave of his New York friends at the City
Hotel. He was then escorted to the steamer James Kent,
by large troops of horse and a battalion of infantry, accompanied by an immense multitude to bid him an affectionate adieu. The boat left the wharf amidst continued
cheers, and the General stood upon deck waving his hat
and hand, and bowing his head until lost to sight by the
multitude on shore.

The General then passed on through New Jersey, Pennsylvania and Maryland, to Washington. Civic and martial honors awaited him all along the route, but must now
be imagined rather than described.

He had a most imposing and cordial welcome at Washington city. Congress was not then in session, but due
honors were paid him by the President, officers of government and citizens. His stay in Washington was then
short, as he intended to return in December, when Congress would be in session.

At noon, on the 16th of September, 1824, he entered
the Ancient Dominion, at Alexandria. Due honors were
paid him here, and he then passed on to Mount Vernon
to pay his devoirs at the shrine of his beloved friend,

Washington. He staid here over Sunday, and on Monday he proceeded down the river Potomac to Yorktown, in company with two other steamers filled with ladies and gentlemen.

His reception at Yorktown was very imposing. The village was turned into a camp, and the veritable tent of Washington was there, into which Lafayette entered with deep emotion, and there received many of his revolutionary friends; and on Wednesday morning he partook of a military breakfast, in the tent of Washington, with his comrades in arms.

After leaving Yorktown the General visited Williamsburg, Norfolk, Petersburg and Richmond. The demonstrations in honor of Gen. Lafayette need not be described in detail, but suffice it to say that all the magnificent parade, splendid decorations, civic feasts and martial honors that marked his whole progress, from the time he first landed on our shores, were displayed to their full extent in the State of Virginia.

General Lafayette left Richmond November 2d, and arrived at Monticello, on a visit to his venerable friend President Jefferson, and arrived there on the 4th. The meeting was most cordial and affectionate. They remained locked in each others' arms several minutes before they could find utterance to their feelings. The General was presented to his family and friends, and was most cordially entertained. He passed a week at Monticello, to enjoy the repose of that beautiful seat, under the courteous hospitality of his beloved friend; and which, also, afforded him some leisure to reply to his numerous correspondents. Although the General had an active and efficient Secretary, yet his unanswered letters then amounted to nearly four hundred!

While here, he visited the University of Virginia, at Charlottsville, some five miles away, and there dined with

5

the faculty of the College, and invited guests. The College was founded by Mr. Jefferson, and he was anxious to attend Lafayette on his visit, but age and ill health prevented. He sent a note, however, apologizing for his absence, and in commendation of his friend.

It may be worthy of note that the Sages of Quincy and Monticello, in about a year and a half after their interview with General Lafayette, both died on the same 4th of July, in 1826; and the messengers who bore tidings of the event, met at Philadelphia, where they had signed the Declaration of Independence together in 1776, just half a century before. Though diverse their lives, during a portion of their long and eventful pilgrimage on earth, they exchanged friendly salutations years before its close, and at last, on the Birthday of the Nation, started for eternity together!

The General then visited President Madison, at Montpelier. His reception there was very cordial; and after a few days he left for Washington City, and arrived there on the 23d of November. He dined on the same day with the President, in company with the officers of the General Government and city.

On a pressing invitation, he visited Baltimore to attend the great Cattle Show of the State of Maryland. He was received at Baltimore with unabated cordiality, and was complimented with the delivery of the premiums. On his return to Washington, he made the White House his headquarters.

When Congress was in session, he was introduced into the Senate by a Committee and most cordially received; but in the House of Representatives he had a most imposing reception.

On Friday, December 10, at one o'clock, he was introduced to the House by a committee of 24 members, and when the General appeared, the members of the House and Senate and distinguished persons admitted on the floor of the House, all rose and remained standing, while Henry Clay, the Speaker, in behalf of Congress and nation, addressed the Nation's Guest, in the highest strains of impassioned eloquence. To which address, Gen. Lafayette replied in a most happy and feeling manner. The House then adjourned, and each member, preceded by the Speaker, took the General by the hand and gave him a hearty welcome. So cordial and fervent was the greeting, that those who witnessed it aver its parallel cannot be found in Grecian or Roman history.

The scene in the Senate was less imposing, but not less honorable; for it is known, that General Lafayette is the only person that ever had a public reception in that body.

On the 22d day of December, 1824, Congress passed a bill granting General Lafayette two hundred thousand dollars in money, and also, a township of public land to be selected by the President. President Munroe selected, it is said, what is now called Tallahassee, in Florida. The President personally presented the land warrant, with an appropriate address. Capitalists then offered General Lafayette one hundred thousand dollars for his township; and as he did not wish to colonize it himself, or sell it by piecemeal, he accepted the offer. He had then three hundred thousand dollars in money, which he deposited in the United States Bank at Philadelphia.

General Lafayette took his tour from Washington through the Southern and Western States about the first of March, 1825. He visited the principal towns in North and South Carolina, Georgia, Alabama, Mississippi, Tennessee, Missouri, Kentucky, Illinois, Indiana and Ohio. He passed up the Mississippi river in a steamer, and then up the Ohio river to Pittsburg. He visited Buffalo, Niagara Falls, and returned to Albany by way of the Erie canal. From Albany he proceeded directly to Boston, through Springfield and Worcester, and arrived there on the 16th day of June, 1825.

On his return to the East, he had visited all the States in the Union, except the two New England States, Maine and Vermont. But he met his revolutionary friend Gov. Eustis no more. He had gone to his rest on the 6th of February before. Gov. Brooks had also died during his absence.

On the 17th day of June, 1825, General Lafayette appeared on Bunker Hill, laid the corner stone of the Bunker Hill Monument, sat on the platform, surrounded by such a civic and military display as is seldom seen among men; and with a sea of upturned faces, listened to the eloquent address of Daniel Webster on that memorable occasion.

Massachusetts had indicated what might be done, by the splendid display on Boston Common, the year before; but it seems it was only a prelude to what her people could do. Bunker Hill was, indeed, captured as never before.

The celebration of the *Fiftieth Anniversary* of the battle of BUNKER HILL, and the ceremony of laying the corner stone of an *Obelisk* to commemorate that great event, took place on the 17th of June, 1825.

A Grand Procession was formed on Boston Common with the utmost precision, under the direction of General Lyman. The military escort was composed of sixteen companies of infantry and a troop of horse, all volunteers and in full uniform. The survivors of the battle followed in eight carriages, about 40 in number; each wearing a badge, "Bunker Hill, June 17." Then some two hundred officers and soldiers of the revolution, with appropriate badges. Then the Bunker Hill Monument Association in full numbers. The Masonic procession succeeded, exceeding two thousand of the fraternity,

with all their jewels and regalia. They were followed by
the Grand Encampments of the Knights Templar of
Rhode Island, Connecticut, Vermont, Maine, New Hampshire and Massachusetts, in full numbers, with banners
and implements. And the Grand Lodges of the above
named States, and by Royal Arch Masons, and by various
subordinate Chapters and Lodges. A full band of music
was attached to the Masonic procession.

Hon. Mr. Webster, Orator of the Day, and President
of the Bunker Hill Association; the other officers.

The Rev. Dr. Kirkland, Rev. Mr. Thaxter and Rev.
Mr. Walker, Chaplain of the Day.

The Directors and Committees of the Association.
Gen. Lafayette in an open coach and four, with General
Lallemand of Philadelphia.

The General's son, George Washington Lafayette, and
the General's suite, in a carriage.

His Excellency the Governor.

The Council, Senate, and House of Representatives.

Governor Fenner of Rhode Island; the Secretary of
War, James Barbour, and others.

Delegations from the several States.

Delegations from the Plymouth Society in Plymouth.

Officers of the Army and Navy, in uniform.

Citizens.

In this order, the whole proceeded through several
streets of Boston, to Monument Square in Charlestown.
The procession was over two miles long, and the front
had reached Charlestown bridge when the rear left the
Common.

On arriving at the ground, General Lafayette, at the
request of Mr. Webster, President of the Association,
assumed a mason's apron, took a trowel in hand, placed
the mortar underneath the prepared corner stone, and by
the assistance of operative masons laid it in its proper

place. Various articles were placed in a box, sealed up and put underneath the stone. A long inscription had been prepared and afterwards put on the Monument itself. By that it appears that John Quincy Adams was President of the United States; Levi Lincoln, Governor of Massachusetts; James Fenner, of Rhode Island; Oliver Wolcott, of Connecticut; David L. Morrill, of New Hampshire; Albion K. Paris, of Maine; and Cornelius P. Van Ness, of Vermont.

The platform was of the most ample dimensions, one-half of which was occupied by more than a thousand ladies. Odes were said and sung, and toasts given. The dinner was given under an edifice erected for the purpose, in which were 12 tables 400 feet long, on which were 4000 plates, and all occupied.

To wind up the ceremonies of the day, Mr. Webster arose, and after a few well chosen prefatory remarks, gave as a toast—

"Health and long life to *General Lafayette.*"

General Lafayette arose and made a few impressive and feeling remarks, and then gave the following sentiment;

"BUNKER HILL, and the holy resistance to oppression, which has already enfranchised the American hemisphere. The next half century jubilee toast shall be *Enfranchised Europe.*"

According to arrangements made the previous year, the General's next excursion was to New Hampshire. And here began my active part in the movements of Gen. Lafayette. On Tuesday, the 21st day of June, 1825, I was in Boston, fully equipped to escort Gen. Lafayette and suite to the Capital of New Hampshire. I had ascertained that besides the General there were his son, George Washington Lafayette, Emile Lavossiur, his private secretary, and his servant — who seemed to be a very capable "man of all work." My equipage consisted of three carriages—a barouche, drawn by four horses, a four-horse stage coach, and a two-horse covered carriage for baggage.. The barouche was precisely the thing needful for the occasion. It was of ample dimensions, the driver's seat was elevated and detached from the body of the carriage, and that swung so low on thorough braces that a person sitting down inside would be no higher than standing up outside. Very convenient, indeed, for shaking hands and presenting children. The carriages and relays of horses on the road had been provided by Mr. Nathaniel Walker, the regular stage-driver on the route from Boston to Concord, N. H. Thus equipped, and ready to call for the General at his lodgings, I was met by the Governor's aid, who said the Governor had concluded that the honor of the State required that he should escort the General, in his own equipage, to the line of the State at Methuen, and we could receive him there without material delay. There did not seem to be anything else to do then but to start at once, and keep out of the way of the Governor's escort.

Just at this moment a revolutionary soldier from Vermont, having attended the Bunker Hill celebration, and having accidentally been left by the stage, begged for a ride as far as Concord on his way home. As I had ample accommodations, he was cheerfully taken on board with me in the barouche. I was not aware of the dilemma I was in until we approached Malden. Then it was that I could see a great crowd in the village, the bells began to ring, cannons were fired, and bands of music cheered, and as we came near could distinctly hear the shouts of "Welcome Lafayette." I then perceived that the multitude believed the soldier at my side was none other than Gen. Lafayette, and were bound to give him due honors. I, therefore, urged the driver to push his team into the midst of the crowd, so that I could undeceive them. With mingled emotions, hard to be described, I arose in the carriage and with great earnestness exclaimed, "'See that you do it not;' the gentleman at my side is *not* Gen. Lafayette, but a soldier of the revolution, accidentally left by the stage, and I am giving him a ride on his way home. I came to Boston, fully equipped to take the General there, but the Governor has otherwise ordered. His escort, with Gen. Lafayette aboard, in all the pomp and circumstance of a triumph, will be here in about an hour. But as your patriotism is up, and this gentleman at my side, no doubt, is a worthy revolutionary soldier, give him three cheers if you please, and we pass on." They did this with a will; the soldier arose, gave a soldier's salute, and we left.

I then began to realize the task I had before me, and had my anticipations more than realized by the time I arrived at Methuen, for I suppose I made more than twenty speeches to the gatherings at the villages, hotels, stores and cross-roads on the route, and Methuen itself was aroused and had to be quieted.

At length my speeches began to be irksome to myself, and I tried to introduce variations, but it was of no avail; for the subject could not be changed, and a mere change of words was no relief. I then began to realize the task imposed on Gen. Lafayette. He had been here nearly a year, making speeches all over the land—often the same in substance, and sometimes nearly in the same words. And his task was double that of mine, for he had to listen to speeches as well as make them, and long, tedious speeches seem to be more irksome to hear than to make.

It has been suggested to me that I might have put the revolutionary soldier in the coach behind me, let down the curtains and avoided all further trouble. But honor and patriotism forbade. He was delighted where he was, bore his "blushing honors" with great complacency, although unwittingly bestowed; and to have placed him in a rear carriage, merely to keep him out of sight, would have been an insult to his dignity. Nor would it have availed, for the stage driver, Walker, had so thoroughly advertised his coming with Gen. Lafayette for more than a week, that the people had assembled along the road, and awaited his coming. And when they saw the portly, honest Walker, driving a barouche, drawn by four horses with flags in their headstalls, and two carriages behind, they would not believe he was making a fool of himself and made all this show for nothing, but that the veritable General must be somewhere aboard, if not readily seen. So that, in fact, demonstrations would have been made had our soldier been invisible.

But one suggestion has been made that pains me to state: palm off our soldier to the multitude as the veritable Gen. Lafayette, and they would have been as well satisfied as if they had seen the real General himself. As our soldier was about seventy years of age, of venerable appearance, and well clad, it might, perhaps, have been done with success. But, setting aside its dishonesty, it would not have been good policy, for in time it would have been known, and woe be to the one that did it—better have a millstone about his neck, and cast into the depths of the sea.

But one thing might have been successfully done—wait for the Governor's escort, and follow in its wake. But this I was not inclined to do, as I had no sympathy with it. I preferred making my monotonous speeches, and these could be short; and I was not compelled to endure the still more irksome task of hearing any speeches in reply.

In about an hour and a half the General arrived at Methuen; and after a half hour of hand-shaking, salutes and speeches, our carriages were at the door, all aboard, and we on our way. My soldier then took a seat in the stage coach, and the General in the barouche with me.

Immediately, I stated to the General the dilemma I had been in, and the many speeches I had to make on account of his absence; but as he was now present, I felt entirely relieved, for I should only be required to hear speeches, and not make them. He laughed heartily at the joke the Governor had unwittingly put upon me, and then said, that he too had made many speeches on the route to Methuen—perhaps not so many in number as I had, for at some of the crossings, where a few only assembled, he only tendered his thanks, and passed on; but he supposed that some of his might have been longer, especially at Andover; but he was willing to call speech-making even; and now, as you have got your hand in, why not alternate me in speech-making on the remainder of the route to Concord? This was said with such a comical face, that I could not but join him in a hearty laugh; for it was well known to him, as well as myself, that the desire to see and hear *him* was so intense that the most eloquent man that ever lived would not be tolerated a moment as his substitute.

Our acquaintance, thus facetiously begun, was continued in a free, frank and easy manner; on the route, at Pembroke, where we staid over night, and at all convenient times at Concord. We had some most glorious chats; for he seemed to enjoy his relief from public speeches and receptions. I was then in the full glow of early manhood, and delighted with him; and when he found I was really interested in him and his, freely imparted all I wished to know. He had a keen eye to all he saw, and gave attention to all he heard, yet we found time for interesting chats about revolutionary times, his family, and his trip through the country. On my part, I was the editor of a newspaper at Concord, and fairly posted in the affairs of the State and Nation, and could generally give him all the information he desired. He wished to know about the reception at Concord, and what was expected of him; and I gave him all the desired information.

We found the scenes on the route in Massachusetts reproduced in New Hampshire; for at all the hotels, stores, villages and cross-roads, multitudes had assembled to greet him as he came. It was in the rosy month of June, and roses were abundant, especially in and about our carriage, in the shape of wreaths and bouquets. At times, our carriage became so much encumbered, that we had to throw them overboard—in solitary places.

When about to meet a crowd for the first time, I asked for instructions. He said, "I wish you would speak to the driver to move slow in this crowd; stop near the centre, and not start till bidden." I can only say that, all along the route, he was greeted by men, women and children; and babies were presented for him to take in his arms and kiss. At one place, a comely, middle-aged lady became so enthusiastic that she pressed forward, put her arm around his neck and gave him a fervent kiss on the cheek. The General, nothing daunted, returned the compliment. Two things I recollect—one was, that I had no objection to be in the General's place; and the other was, that the air rung with loud shouts of applause. All along the route, the General would rise in his carriage, wave his hat, and return thanks for the attentions shown him; but he made no formal address until he reached Concord.

At Derry Centre Village, the Rev. Dr. Dana was introduced to him; and at his request, the General visited a ladies' school near by, kept by Miss Grant. The Doctor introduced the General to the teacher and spoke a few words in regard to the school. A hundred and one fair,

fresh and healthy young ladies composed the school, all
dressed alike, each having on a white dress, a blue sash
around the waist, and a full-blown rose in the hair. They
all arose when we entered, and, at a signal, formed round
in single file before the General; and each one, as her
name was announced by the teacher, took him by the
hand. The General made a few remarks in commendation of the teacher and scholars, and we retired.

As we came out to our carriage, an excited youth was
ringing the meeting-house bell with all his might, and at
the same time intensely gazing at the General; but as we
passed on, he could not keep the bell-rope in hand and see
the General. He then, dropped the rope and stood out
with lifted hands, intensely gazing. But the bell stopped.
The General shook his sides and said : "That boy thinks
the bell is as enthusiastic as he is, and will keep on ringing while he is looking."

We were to dine at the Hotel in the lower village of
Derry, on the turnpike, a mile away. When we came to
the brow of the hill overlooking the village, we beheld
what an excited clergyman might call "a section of the
day of judgment." Small and great were indeed there,
forming a multitude far exceeding anything we had seen
on the route. As we approached, the cannon on the hill
beyond began to utter their deep-toned voices; bands
played, flags waved, and the sound of many voices was
heard in shouts of welcome. The Irish blood was up,
and ringing voices betokened healthy lungs, and the shouts
were overwhelming.

The crowd gave way as we approached the door of the
Hotel, and we entered. While we were in the wash-room,
a message came that the feelings of the people were so
intense to see the General, that they begged to see him
before he sat down to dinner. As he consented, we went
out on to the upper porch, and I announced GENERAL

LAFAYETTE. The shout was repeated, if possible louder than before; and when we were about to retire, a revolutionary veteran stepped out a pace or two in front of the crowd, and with a loud voice made an impromptu speech. The General made a short reply, bowed, and took his leave. At the table, the General said, that was one of the best speeches he had heard since he came to America—short, pungent, patriotic, and to the point.

The Hall was large, and tables all full; and many of the yeomanry had the pleasure of dining with General Lafayette.

Our route lay through Suncook Village, at the South end of Pembroke. There, Major Caleb Stark, son of Major General John Stark, lived; and as he had a slight acquaintance with General Lafayette in the revolutionary war, had written to him a request that he would call at his house, as he very much wished to see him and introduce him to his family. We called, and on introducing him to the General, he seized his hand, and began an animated speech about revolutionary times, which did not seem soon to terminate. His family was standing on the opposite side of the room waiting to be introduced; but he seemed to have forgotten them. I was acquainted with the Major, but not with his family, and could not introduce them myself. In this dilemma, the spirited Miss Harriet Stark, no longer able to brook delay, came forward, seized General Lafayette's hand, and said: "Permit me to introduce myself to you as the eldest daughter of Maj. Caleb Stark, with whom you are talking, and the grand-daughter of Major-General John Stark, the hero of Bennington; and now, permit me to introduce you to my mother, brothers and sisters;" which she did, with her usual promptness and energy.

When we were seated in the carriage, Gen. Lafayette said: "Miss Harriet Stark does indeed inherit all the fire

and spirit of her grandfather, and would have been a
heroine had she lived in the exciting scenes of revolutionary times."

Near the close of a beautiful summer's day, one of the
longest in the year, we entered upon the long main street
of Pembroke. The sun, having moved round his long
circle in the sky, was resting in crimson robes on the
Western hills, and soon retired for the night. Not so
Pembroke village; that was wide awake, and gave the
General as enthusiastic a welcome as he had received anywhere on the route. Sometimes, it seemed, the less the
numbers the greater the zeal.

We had used due diligence and travelled rapidly when
not hindered; but our coming had been so well advertised
by the well-known Walker, the stage driver on the route,
that it was known to all people, far and near. And so it
was, that we were not only detained at villages, hotels
and cross-roads, but even at a single cottage. Our approach seemed to have been watched; and, at the report
of a musket or bugle blast, people would rapidly appear
from their lounging places, where none were visible before; and the General must needs pause a moment, take
by the hand those near by, and speak a few words. Infancy and age were alike presented, and the halt and the
lame were sitting in easy chairs before the cottage doors.
At one of these cottages an invalid old lady, "cadaverous
and pale," was brought by two men, in her armed chair,
to the carriage; she seized the General's hand with both
of hers, and with tearful eyes, exclaimed "Bless the
Lord!"

At Fiske's hotel, on the Main street of Pembroke, five
miles from Concord, we rested for the night. A large
concourse of people gave the General a hearty welcome,
and shook hands with him, and he made a short speech.
On my suggesting to the most active men, that the Gen-

eral had had a long and fatiguing day, and needed rest; the people promptly retired, and Pembroke village could never have been more quiet.

After supper, the General leaned back in his easy chair, and said he should sleep better if he sat up an hour before retiring for the night; and he agreed that I might sit up with him and have a pleasant chat. I did but little more than make suggestions and ask questions, all of which he readily and courteously answered. The conversation related to himself, family, revolutionary times, and his trip through the country. So interested I became, that I took no note of time, and am fearful that I kept him up too long; but he did not seem to be weary or impatient. Of this, and other conversations I had with him, I shall allude to before I close; but I recollect our evening's conversation wound up by his saying that I was the most inquisitive man he had found in America; but I seemed so much interested in him and his, that it was with pleasure he had given me the information I desired.

Wednesday, June 22, 1825, was the memorable day of his reception at Concord. A committee of the Legislature, consisting of Stephen P. Webster, of the Senate, and four members of the House, came down in a coach and six to escort the General to Concord. Six white horses were attached to our barouche, Mr. Webster and the General aboard, and I took a seat in the stage coach with George Washington Lafayette. The procession started, and a long line of carriages followed. The procession was met at the lower end of the Dark Plains, opposite the lower bridge over the Merrimac river, by twenty Independent Companies of New Hampshire Militia, the whole commanded by Gen. Bradbury Bartlett, of Nottingham, and the two wings by Gen. Joseph Towle of Epping, and Col. William Kent, of Concord. After the usual salutes and evolutions, the procession proceeded

under this escort, over the bridge, up Main street, around
the old North Church, down State street to Pleasant
street, down Pleasant street to Main street again, and up
Main street to the gate of the State House yard. The
General was then escorted to the Hall of the House of
Representatives, in which were assembled the Governor,
Council, Senate, Members of the House, Officers of the
State, and invited guests, while the gallery was filled with
ladies.

Gen. Lafayette was introduced to Governor Morrill by
Hon. Edmund Parker, of Amherst, Chairman of the Committee of Arrangements. Gov. Morrill arose, and gave
him a cordial welcome in behalf of the Government and
people of the State. To this the General very appro-
priately replied; and here all formality was ended, and
each individual took him by the hand.

In the area below, two hundred and ten revolutionary
soldiers, with Gen. Benjamin Pierce at their head, were
assembled to pay their respects to Gen. Lafayette. He
was introduced to Gen. Pierce, and then he introduced
him to each individual soldier. It was a slow process,
and very affecting, for all shed tears, and some of them
"sobbed aloud." Some of them were recognized as his
companions in arms; among whom was Lieut. Robert
Wilkins, of Concord. He reminded the General of a
perilous foraging expedition performed at his request,
which he remembered, and added some particulars that
the modesty of the Lieutenant had omitted.

After the General had been introduced to them all, he
came up to the centre of the line, and gave them a few
most affectionate parting words. There was not a dry
eye in the room; and although I was only a looker on, I
could not restrain my emotions.

The General was then escorted to the dwelling house
of Col. William A. Kent, on Pleasant street, which was

his headquarters while in Concord. This house was then the handsomest in the village, but it seems, it is removed, and a more modern building occupies its place.

On the same day, a public dinner was given in honor of the General, under an awning in the State House yard, furnished by John P. Goss of the Columbian Hotel, at which the revolutionary soldiers were invited and attended in a body.

At this feast, speeches were made, toasts were drank and songs were sung. A volunteer toast was given by Gov. Morrill, another by Gen. Lafayette, and a third by his son. Two patriotic songs were furnished for the occasion—one by Col. Phillip Carigain of Concord, and the other by Moses L. Neal, Esq., of Dover; and both were well sung by John D. Abbott of Concord. But of the incidents and enthusiasm of this feast, why need I speak? Concord and the State did their duty fully, leaving nothing to be regretted or desired.

Many conventions have been held at Concord. It has been honored by the visits of five Presidents of the United States—Washington, Munroe, Jackson, Polk and Grant; and it witnessed the great "log cabin" display of 1840; but never was seen, on any other occasion, such a public display and deep-toned enthusiasm as attended the reception of Gen. Lafayette. Words are inadequate to describe it; and could it be done, the present generation would hardly comprehend or believe it.

Concord was then full of people, and it could hold more then than now, for there were more vacant lots and fewer houses. The streets were running over, and the vacant lots were full of shanties, awnings and people. The two cannons on the hill back of the State House vied with each other to see which could speak the loudest without bursting; and the solitary church bell of the old North rang out its merriest peal; and although it found no answering voice in kind, yet the martial music, shouts of men and roar of cannon kept it in countenance and cheered it on.

The General took tea with Governor Morrill at his residence, dropped in to hear the N. H. Musical Society a few moments, and then attended a grand levee in the area of the State House and State House yard. The Capitol and surrounding buildings were illuminated, and a vast throng attended.

At this levee, I introduced my wife and first-born child to the General, and announced his name to be George Washington. He shook hands with the wife, took the child in his arms, impressed a kiss on its cheek, looked at the mother, and then at the child; and in a subdued, "still small voice," said: "I am reminded of the loved and the lost!" I knew it reminded him of his own beloved wife; his first-born child; and his noble friend Washington—*all dead!* So impressive was the scene, that the mother wept as well as himself, and could not speak of it in after life without tears. An impulsive man of strong sympathies, like Lafayette, must needs have deep sorrows, as well as great joys.

The evening wound up by another levee at Col. W. A. Kent's. This was designed more especially for the accommodation of the ladies and gentlemen of Concord. The house, street and surrounding buildings were so well illuminated that it was as light as day in and around it. I stood in the ample portico by the hour to see the anxious throng pressing forward to take by the hand and pay their respects to the Nation's Guest. Men, women and children, high, low, rich and poor, with one intent, came and went in one continuous throng till late into night. It was interesting to see the contrast between the comers and goers. The comers pressed forward with hurried step and anxious face; while the goers moved along with quiet step and satisfied air to their respective homes. This remarkable levee was more than half a century ago, and few indeed survive that attended it.

The next morning, the General took his departure for Portland, Maine. He was escorted by Col. Andrew Pierce of Dover, a member of the Senate, and Col. William Smith of Exeter, one of the Governor's aids. He went by the way of Northwood and Durham, stopped at Dover over night, at the mansion of Hon. William Hale; and the next day, went as far as Saco. He entered Portland early on Saturday morning, staid there over night, and at 7 o'clock Sunday morning, he quietly left, on his return trip. He came back the same way he went, and staid at Northwood Sunday night. On Monday forenoon, at 10 o'clock, he passed through the main street of Concord again and dined at the Phœnix Hotel. In all his trip, due honors were paid him, and his receptions were most cordial and enthusiastic; can well be imagined and need not be described.

On an interview with him, he inquired if I had published an account of his reception at Concord; and being answered in the affirmative, he requested a copy, and said, he had obtained as many of the accounts of his visits as he well could, so that, on his return to France, he might live the scenes over again, and call to mind the many valued friends he had left behind. On handing him a copy, he gave it to his Secretary; and so, I suppose, a copy of the "New Hampshire Statesman" is quietly resting in the library of Lagrange.

On Monday, June 27, 1825, a six-horse stage coach for General Lafayette and suite, and a two-horse carriage for baggage, were at the front yard gate of the Capitol. I staid by the carriages, while the General went up into the State House to take leave of the Legislature, then in session. While he was gone, a controversy arose who should drive General Lafayette. It was deemed such an honor to drive a carriage with the General aboard, that it was sought for with great zeal. It appeared that the Northern line out of Concord, having the newest and most elegant coach, had furnished that; and the Southern line, by which he was to travel, had furnished the horses. Through the intervention of the stage agent, a compromise was made—the Northern man should drive one relay of horses, and the Southern man the remainder of the route.

Just at this time, Dr. Dixi Crosby of Gilmanton, afterwards professor at Hanover, came in great haste to be introduced to the General before his departure. I went with him to the State House, and met the General at the steps. After an introduction, we passed down the walk to the carriages. The General put his arm around me, pressed me to his side, gave a cordial invitation to visit Lagrange, took his seat in the coach, waved his hand, and I saw him no more. Let it not be supposed that the General took leave of me in a manner unusual to him; for that was his mode of taking leave where he had become well acquainted; and was precisely the way he took leave of the Massachusetts Governor's aid at Methuen.

The driver on the box of a splendid coach, six elegant horses and harnesses to match, flags each side of the stage box and flags on the horses' head-stalls, with Gen Lafayette aboard, stretched himself up proudly erect, gathered up his ribbons, six in hand, cracked his whip and was off at a bound. It seemed that the horses felt the excitement of the hour, for they bounded down Main street, up Pleasant street, and over the Asylum Hill at full speed, and soon were lost to sight.

The General's route lay through Hopkinton, Warner and Claremont in New Hampshire, and Windsor, Montpelier and Burlington in Vermont. He spent the Fourth of July at Albany, took a steamer for the city of New

York, and from thence went to Washington City. John Quincy Adams was then President of the United States, and on his invitation General Lafayette made his home at the White House, to rest, for rest he really needed after taking such an exciting and laborious tour through the 24 States of the Union. A Roman General might well endure a triumph for a day; but who can stand a triumph for hundreds of days in succession?

When the General signified his desire to return to France, the new frigate Brandywine, named in honor of the battle of Brandywine, in which he bravely fought and was wounded, was brought round to the Navy Yard at Washington, fully equipped for sea, and all things needful for his comfort put on board. It was a new ship, just finished, and had never tried its wings on the ocean.

On the 6th day of September, 1825, the birthday of General Lafayette, at the Eastern steps of the White House, President John Quincy Adams, in presence of the officers of the Government and a vast concourse of ladies and gentlemen, bid the Nation's Guest a final farewell, in one of the most touching and eloquent addresses that had been delivered to him in all his travels through the United States. The next day the vessel put to sea, and in due time arrived safely in France. His reception was most cordial—far different from the manner of his leaving; for the King of France had learned that he was a man of too much importance to be trifled with or abused. But retributive justice, in time, was measurably done; for the arrogant King, who abused when he could, and decently treated when he must, in the three days' revolution of 1830 was deprived of his power, despised and disowned, and had to flee his country to save his own life. General Lafayette's family met him at Havre, where he landed, and his tenants flocked round him as he drew near Lagrange, and gave him a most cordial welcome.

Thus came and thus went the gallant hero, General Lafayette. It seems, that he left France in a private vessel, empty handed, insulted and oppressed; and returned in a national ship, with flags of two great nations flying at the main peak, mizzen and fore, heavy laden and triumphant.

As General Lafayette came here on the 15th of August, 1824, and returned on the 8th of September, 1825, he remained here one year and twenty-three days. Strike off the 23 days as his Sabbath of rest, and it was more than that; and as the number of States was then 24, just double the months in a year, it would give him just half a month to visit each State, provided he equally divided his time. But as the larger States, like New York and Virginia, required more than his average time, he could devote but a few days to the smaller states. He devoted less than a week each to Maine, New Hampshire and Vermont.

But when it is considered that he continually visited schools, academies, factories, public buildings, libraries, legislatures, and many of the curiosities of the country; and then went through a continual round of receptions, dinners and speeches, and travelled thousands of miles over this extended country, often in stage coaches, over hills and rough roads, it is a marvel that he visited the twenty-four States of the Union in the time and manner he did, and live. There were, indeed, steamboats and canal boats in those days, and he occasionally made use of them on the Eastern and Western waters; but not to any great extent, as they did not often move in the direction he wished to travel. And during all this time he carried on a voluminous correspondence, which caused him not a little trouble and fatigue, notwithstanding he had the services of an efficient private secretary.

While he was here he had the pleasure of hearing some

of our greatest orators of the time — Henry Clay, at Washington city; Prof. Edward Everett, at Cambridge College, Daniel Webster, at Bunker Hill, and last, though not least, President John Quincy Adams, at the Capitol. Many other patriotic and eloquent speeches he must have heard, as well as many tedious and dull ones. But many speeches, tedious or otherwise, addressed to him day after day, and to which he must needs make a reply, must have been exceedingly trying to the nerves, and it is a marvel that he sustained himself as well as he did.

Thus far, I have endeavored to give my recollections of General Lafayette's visit to this country in 1824 and '25. It is more than half a century ago, and I have to trust to my minutes, memory, and recollections of others; and may, therefore, be sometimes mistaken in my facts; yet the exciting scenes of the time are so strongly impressed on my mind that most of the transactions here recited seem as fresh and vivid as the events of yesterday. I was then, as now, a great admirer of General Lafayette. I deem him one of the greatest patriots of the age in which he lived; yea, one of the greatest patriots of any age. *We* fought for our own country, firesides and friends. *He* left the the warm precincts of Lagrange, a beautiful and beloved wife, and against the remonstrance of friends and king, fitted out a vessel at his own expense, and sailed three thousand miles away to fight the battles of another country, struggling for existence and against powerful odds. He could not hope for fame — hardly success; and yet he hazarded his life, spent his substance and time, most disinterestedly and nobly, throughout our Revolution, without compensation or reward. No wonder at the great enthusiasm at his presence, for not a few at that day knew of his great services and merits. And should I be accused of exaggeration in describing the scenes of the time, I can only say, that I feel, language is all too poor fully to describe the scenes as they actually occurred.

I turn back half a century in the course of time, and imagine myself standing in the presence of Lafayette; and the exciting scenes pass in rapid review before me; and hear, or seem to hear, the shouts of welcome along the streets, and the booming of cannon echoing from the surrounding forests and hills. And I feel much like the veteran soldier of many battles, who recounts the perilous conflicts of early days, and stretches up his unpliant limbs, "shoulders his crutch to show how fields are won." Will it be said that words and sounds are wind? Granted, but wind is one of the most powerful elements of nature—it prostrates forests and tears to atoms the dwellings of men. Let him that doubts the potency of sound turn to the Bible and there learn that the tooting of ramshorns tumbled down the walls of Jericho.

If any young man desires to live a useful life and perform noble deeds, in spite of all opposition, let him unbuckle his vest, expand his chest, inflate his lungs, and give an explosion worthy of the days of Layayette. No one knows his powers till he tries them, and noble deeds are never done without an attempt.

The triumphant tour of Gen. Lafayette through all the States of the Union, at the time and under the circumstances, was the most remarkable in the history of the world. President Munroe was the last of revolutionary heroes, and the people were much divided in regard to his successor. Members of Congress nominated William H. Crawford, of Georgia; conventions in the States nominated John Quincy Adams of Massachusetts, Henry Clay of Kentucky, and Gen. Andrew Jackson of Tennessee—four candidates, and all alike professed republicans; the contest was, therefore, more personal than political, and spirited, sharp, and oftentimes severe. The election, in November, resulted in no choice by the people; and the House of Representatives, voting by States, elected John

Quincy Adams by a majority of one vote, he having 13 out of the 24, and was inaugurated President on the 4th of March, 1825. Now, during this severe conflict, Gen. Lafayette visited the United States, and passed through the entire Union in such a succession of triumphs that never had been conferred on mortal man before. And this was entirely universal; not a discordant voice was heard; for the presence of Gen. Lafayette, like oil on the troubled waters, hushed to rest the strife of partisan zeal, and all joined together as one man, and gave him all the glory and honor they had the ability to bestow. And this was not mere adulation or outside show, often rendered to office and power; but from deep, heartfelt emotions; and to a man who had neither office, patronage nor power. And those who are inclined to despair of the Republic, can turn with pride and hope to this bright page in our history and be comforted.

And now, I proceed to relate some of the conversations I had with Gen. Lafayette. When I suggested to him that he had made so many patriotic speeches himself, and so many had been made to him with his approbation, and these would be published in France and come to the knowledge of the King, might he not, under some plausible pretext, confiscate his three hundred thousand dollars and imprison him. "Ah, sir," said he, "I am well provided against that: I have deposited the three hundred thousand dollars in the United States Bank at Philadelphia, there to remain, subject to my draft, and will be drawn only as fast as I wish to use it. The Bank has agreed to allow me six per cent. on the money, and send it as I wish to use it, without expense to me. Therefore, the King cannot touch *that* if so disposed. And as to annoying or imprisoning me, I have *now* no fears of that; for by the time I shall have returned to France he will be well aware of the estimation in which I am held by my

8

American friends, and that they will not see me abused. If the King should make an attack on me, my American friends would rise en masse and vindicate my rights; and a war with America would dethrone him; for the American trade is all important to the manufactures of France. I shall, therefore, return to France an independent man, financially and politically; for my funds he *cannot* touch, and my person he *dare* not."

I then inquired of him if these many great public displays which he had witnessed for nearly a year, in which he had taken such an active part, had not, in a measure, affected his health, and whether a less rapid movement might not have been less fatiguing. He replied that rapid movement was his nature, and his military education had confirmed it as a habit. It was more irksome to a spirited horse to be put under the curb than to take his own natural gait. He had, however, been compelled to travel faster, and more in the night, than was agreeable to him; but he wished to fulfil all his engagements if he could; and it was unpleasant to feel that multitudes ahead were anxiously awaiting his arrival. But delays were unavoidable, and the best arrangements failed of performance, where men, women and children were in the programme; for they could not be handled with the precision and promptness of a military company; but he felt that all the executive officers had done their duty to the utmost, and rendered his visits as pleasant as possible. On the whole, fatiguing or otherwise, he had enjoyed his trip greatly, and the delightful scenes through which he had passed could never be effaced from his memory.

But he had learned something by experience; toned down his feelings and improved every opportunity for rest. The display at New York took him entirely by surprise, especially in extent; and was in such contrast to his leaving France, that for a time, he was completely overwhelmed, and felt the effects of it afterwards. But since then, he had so much disciplined himself that he had witnessed displays as imposing, if not as extensive, with composure and joy. Perhaps he had over-estimated his power of endurance ; but he felt that he should finish his tour without materially impairing his constitution, and when he had taken his rest, find himself in his usual fair health.

In 1784, more than forty years before, he had visited his American friends, and had a most cordial and enthusiastic reception ; but that was immediately after a successful revolution ; and he met many comrades in war, as well as personal friends, and an enthusiastic meeting might be expected ; but after a generation had passed, and few personal friends remained, he did not expect anything more than a generous and quiet welcome. He could not fully comprehend how services rendered nearly half a century before, disinterested and patriotic as they might be, should cause such an enthusiastic display by a people, generally, strangers to him, and in the heat of an excited canvass for the election of a President of the United States. He had attended these enthusiastic receptions for nearly a year, and had not yet fully solved the problem. Although, like the human countenance, they were similar, yet distinguishable from each other. It had been gratifying, as well as surprising, to witness what the ingenuity of the American people could do ; and yet, there seemed to be so much affection, gratitude and kindness behind it all, he did not feel himself worthy of so much homage. Nor could he claim or appropriate all the honors to himself, but must attribute much to the cause he advocated, and the great love of liberty which characterized the American people.

He also spoke of the appearance of the country, and the great contrast between his going and coming. Although he had taken American newspapers, and made many inquiries of his American visiting friends, yet he could truly say, the half had not been told him. In 1784, when he left this country, neither Florida nor Louisiana had been annexed, and the long tier of States on the East side of the Mississippi river did not exist as States, and were scarcely inhabited by civilized man; and Washington City itself was a wilderness. He was surprised at the rapid improvement throughout the Western country, and the Eastern did not lag much behind. He marvelled greatly at the city of Rochester, in the State of New York. He said he found in the revolutionary woods a great city, so rapidly and recently built, that the very founders were the men talking to him.

Although he had spent some of the best days of his life in aiding the American people to gain their independence, he regretted it not, but felt more than amply paid for all his toils and troubles, in witnessing its noble results. In travelling over the States of the Union, he had found improvements far beyond all his expectations, and an intelligent, prosperous and happy people. The first thing he noticed on his arrival, was the absence of squalid poverty, the canaille, sans culottes or rabble, such a prominent and disagreeable feature in Europe, when the people assemble *en masse* on great occasions. One great attractive feature in the public displays, was the school children, who appeared by hundreds and thousands, especially in the large cities, who were neatly clad, often in uniform, and appeared healthy and happy. It was truly affecting, to hear the joyous shouts of childhood, ringing out shouts of welcome in tones so piercing and shrill, that they could be heard above the din of the hour. And he often paused as he passed, rose in his carriage, and with deep emotion, waved his hat and hand, and bowed his head, in token of his appreciation of their hearty welcomes. He found the great mass of the people, also, well-clad, intelligent and courteous; and, indeed, he felt proud of the country; and could see no reason why it should not improve in the future as in the past, and in time become one of the greatest nations on earth. Thus far, his anticipations have been more than realized; for his 24 States have become 38, the population more than doubled, and the country greatly increased in size, by the addition of the large territories of Texas, New Mexico and California, counting Alaska nothing.

When I signified a wish or desire to know the extent of his sacrifices in the cause of American Independence, he saw at once the drift of my wishes, and said: he came here at first, not to make money, but to spend it. His income was then, counting that of Lagrange with his large estates in the South of France together, more than thirty-seven thousand dollars a year; and he made up his mind to spend every dollar that could be spared in the cause of American Independence. But his income, though ample for an individual, was of but little account in a great war. His greatest services, therefore, he had rendered were in persuading others, especially the Courts of Spain and France, to furnish the needful munitions of war. His importunity sometimes had been so great, that the King of France said to his ministers in his presence, that he thought Lafayette would strip the palace of Versailles of its furniture to clothe the American army; and he curtly replied, "*I would*."

I then said, that a member of Congress had publicly stated, in the House, that he had spent, of his own money, a hundred and forty thousand dollars in the cause of the American revolution, and had never taxed a dollar for his great services in the cause. "Ah, well," he said, "I never stopped to count the dollars; and others may know, perhaps, as much about it as I do; but this I know, that whatever it was, it went freely and never for a moment regretted; but I gloried then, as I do now, that I have made so good a use of what fortune had placed within my control. And as to my own services, whether great or small, I never taxed or received a dollar for them, either in the American or French revolutions."

I then said to him, that in some of his speeches he had said, or intimated, something like a desire or intention of returning to this country and spending the remainder of his days with us. He said that in the excitement of some of his receptions, he had, probably, intimated something of the kind, for it was painful to think of leaving so many valued friends forever, to meet them no more upon earth; but prudence dictated to him the propriety of remaining in the milder climate of France in his old age; nor should he feel so much at home anywhere in the world as at La-grange. And the attachment between himself and family was mutual, and they would never consent to leave France. He had then four children: Anastasia, Virginia and Carolina, his daughters; and George Washington Lafayette, his only son; and a larger number of grand-children. They were all united in one harmonious house-hold, and could not be separated while life lasted. His first-born daughter, Henriette, died while he was here in the American revolution. It was a sad affliction to him; still greater, if possible, to the mother; and he was sorely tempted to return home and comfort her all he could, but stern duties here forbade.

But there were other reasons besides these why he should not reside here. The enthusiasm now was too great to last. In time it must come down to the realities of everyday life. Should he live here, he must have his associates and friends. In a Republic there would always be two parties, at least, and should he join one, he would offend the other; if he joined neither he would offend both. And then, as he had always been a frank and out-spoken man, his position in society might not be altogether pleasant; and he had a feeling that he still might be of some service to his native France.

And, moreover, he should most sadly miss his noble friend, Washington, and his wife. Although he had paid his devoirs at Mount Vernon and " wept full sore" at their tomb, they never could be restored to him upon earth; and he should miss them more here, where he had been accustomed to see them, than at his home in France. No man could feel more grateful than himself for the great favors bestowed and the kind feelings expressed, and he should leave America sorrowing that stern necessity required that he should take a last farewell of so many noble, generous and devoted friends.

His friendship for Washington, he said, could not be expressed by words. It was the friendship of David and Jonathan repeated. Although double his own age, and more sedate and less impulsive, yet their cordial intimacy, in the long and vexing scenes of the revolution, had never been disturbed. Although unlike, they were in agreement with each other. If he had at any time been a spur to Washington, more often he had been a curb to himself. Washington had been censured for his want of energy in the prosecution of the war, but he thought, wrongfully. He could not do as he would for the lack of means, and could not disclose to the public his destitution without informing the enemy also; and at times, had the enemy known his condition, it would have been fatal.

Washington did not lack energy, but it was regulated by prudence. He never made long speeches to his army, or boasted of what he had done, or was about to do; and yet, when thoroughly aroused, the stoutest heart would quail before him. He had been his aid, when he mounted his charger on the eve of a battle, rode round the army, took his position in front, while his soldiers passed in review before him, and then wave an adieu with his hat, and not a word spoken; yet his face would glow with emotion, and his appearance and bearing were more powerful than words. His soldiers understood him, and were ready to fight to the utmost; and woe to the foe they encountered.

General Lafayette's suggestion that he might yet be of some service to his native France seemed rather prophetic, for in the three days' revolution of 1830 he was called to the command of the National Guards, and through his influence Louis Philippe was chosen Citizen King, peace was restored, and the revolution ended without bloodshed. Although the people clamored for a Republic, and would have made him Chief Magistrate, yet he did not deem this best for France; and having no ambition for power, he respectfully but firmly declined.

When speaking of the incidents of the revolutionary war, the General said, one of the most painful duties he had to perform was to sit on the court martial that tried and condemned Major Andre. He appeared to be a gallant officer, and not intentionally a spy; but as he did come within the American lines to induce an American officer to commit treason, he was by military law a spy, and had to be condemned. Gen. Washington was not disposed to deal harshly with him, and permitted him to use his best efforts to get him exchanged for Gen. Arnold; but that proved unsuccessful. Washington signed his death warrant in tears, and appointed the day of his execution. When that arrived, it was postponed in the hope that something would occur to relieve the stern necessity of his execution. As nothing in his favor appeared, Major Andre, at last, was executed on the 2d of October, 1780, and died as he had lived, a brave man. His death was a sad blow to his mother and three sisters; for he

was the favorite of the family, who were mainly depen-
dent on him for support. The King of England, however, granted the mother a pension, which placed them in
comfortable circumstances.

After the war, Gen. Arnold, with his usual effrontery,
called upon the family of Maj. Andre, at their residence,
in London. The answer was crisp: "Good looking, or
otherwise, he could not be admitted; they did not wish to
see a *traitor*." Although the British people accepted the
treason, they despised the *traitor*, and he had no friends
among decent people where he lived, any more than in
his native country.

The General said that Washington, Hamilton and
Knox, as well as himself, had great compassion for Gen.
Arnold's young wife; for they believed her innocent of
the treason. But from an investigation of the subject
since, I think they were all mistaken, for I believe she
was, in fact, the prime mover of the whole matter. And
my reasons are, that she belonged to a decided tory family
in Philadelphia. And when the British army occupied
that city, her father's house was a resort of the British
officers, and they were welcome guests at all times, especially Maj. Andre. Miss Shippen (Arnold's wife) and
Maj. Andre were intimate friends, and much in each
other's company before her marriage, and they corresponded both before and after that event; and, undoubtedly through her, Gen. Arnold was induced to enter into
a negotiation with her early favorite. But what renders
the fact of guilt in the treason certain is her own confes-
sion. On her way to Philadelphia, she stopped at the
residence of Mrs. Prevost, who became the wife of Aaron
Burr, and there confessed the whole matter. She said
she was glad to throw off the mask and assume her true
character before her intimate friend; for she had induced
and helped plan the negotiation with Maj. Andre, and was

9

sadly disappointed at its failure; as, had it been successful, she and her husband would have taken a high position in the British Government, and possessed a fortune.

In regard to Maj. Andre, I inquired of the General if he had any interviews with him, and had learned anything of his early history. He said he had not; other matters of greater importance occupied his time, and he knew nothing in particular in regard to Maj. Andre and his family. I then said I could post him up in the matter to some extent, for in 1821, when the Duke of York caused his remains to be removed from Tappan, and placed in Westminster Abbey, and a mural slab placed there to his memory, I gathered up some fragments of his life, and wrote a short sketch at the time, which was published.

It appeared that Maj. John Andre was born in London, in 1751; but his parents were from Geneva, in Switzerland, and he was sent there for his education. On his return he entered a London counting-house, but at the early age of eighteen he formed a romantic attachment for a beautiful lady by the name of Honora Sneyd, who returned his passion, and they became engaged. But the father of the lady interfered, and the premature match was broken off. Andre then abandoned the counting-house and entered the army. His first commission is dated March 4, 1771, and he went to Germany, and did not return to England till 1773, still haunted by his passion. But, in the meantime, his lady-love had been induced to marry another person, for she had become the second wife of Richard L. Edgeworth, the father of the celebrated Miss Maria Edgeworth. In 1774, Maj. Andre came to America as Lieutenant of the Royal English Fusileers, and was captured early in the war, with other officers, by Gen. Montgomery. After his exchange, he was appointed by Sir Henry Clinton, Adjutant-General of the British army with the rank of Major, and served under him until his death.

His romantic attachment followed him through life, and after his capture, he wrote to a friend that he had been stripped of everything but the miniature of Honora, which he painted in 1769, and which he concealed when he was searched; and added, "possessing that, I yet think myself fortunate." He was personally pleasing, and gentlemanly in his bearing, and naturally of a festive and romantic disposition. He often indulged himself in poetry; much of which seems to have been induced by his early love. He designated himself as Damon, and his lost lady as Delia. In early life I used to hear said, or sung :—

> " Return, enraptured hours,
> " When Delia's heart was mine," &c.

And then again—

> " Ah! Delia, see the fatal hour;
> Farewell, my soul's delight.
> O, how can wretched Damon live,
> When banished from thy sight!"

His varied and graceful talents and engaging manners rendered him a general favorite, both in the army and among the people. He was the prime mover of all the elegant amusements in camp and garrison. He also indulged in writing poetical squibs or lampoons on the American army. His propensity for caricature had recently been indulged in a mock heroic poem, in three cantos, celebrating an attack upon a British picket by Gen. Wayne, and the driving into the American camp a drove of cattle by Lee's dragoons. It was written in great humor and grotesque imagery, and represented that Mad Anthony lost his horse on that "great occasion." Three cantos were printed at different times in Rivingston's Gazette; and it so happened that the last canto was printed the very day of Andre's capture; and ended with the following ominous lines :—

"And now I close my epic strain,
And tremble as I show it ;—
Lest this same warrior-drover Wayne
Should ever catch the poet."

His strong propensity for the ludicrous did not forsake him, even in his prison ; for he amused himself in making a ludicrous sketch of himself and his rustic escort under march, and presented it to the officer in attendance, and pleasantly said, "This will give you an idea of the style in which I had the honor of being conducted to my present abode."

Whether I said all this, less or more, I cannot recollect, but I do remember that the General said in reply that he was a very pleasant, gentlemanly man ; very popular in the American camp as well as in the British, and that he was very frank on his trial—so much so, that it was not needful for the Judge Advocate to produce any witnesses. Hamilton was almost in daily intercourse with him, and deemed him a well educated gentleman, improved by travel, and of some proficiency in poetry, music and the fine arts.

But I do not know how to give the public any better idea of the feelings, public and private, in regard to Maj. Andre, at the time of his trial and execution, than what is contained in a letter from General Tallmadge to Col. Webb, one of Washington's aids. The letter says: "Poor Andre, who has been under my charge almost ever since he was taken, had yesterday his trial ; and though his sentence is not known, a disgraceful death is undoubtedly allotted him. By heavens! Col Webb, I never saw a man whose fate I foresaw, whom I so sincerely pitied. He is a young man of the greatest accomplishments, and was the prime minister of Sir Harry Clinton on all occasions. He has unbosomed his heart to me so fully, and, indeed, let me know almost every motive of his actions since he came out on his late mission, that

he has endeared me to him exceedingly. Unfortunate
man! He will undoubtedly suffer death to-morrow;
and though he knows his fate, seems to be as cheerful as
if he were going to an assembly! I am sure, he will go
to the gallows less fearful for his fate, and with less con-
cern than I shall behold the tragedy. Had he been tried
by a court of ladies, he is so genteel, handsome, polite a
young gentleman, that I am confident they would have
acquitted him. But enough of Maj. Andre, who, though
he dies lamented, falls justly."

" Never has any man, suffering under like circumstances, awakened more universal sympathy, even among those
of the country against which he had practiced, than Maj.
Andre. His story is one of the touching themes of the
revolution; and his name is still spoken of with kindness
in the local traditions of the neighborhood where he was
captured."

What a contrast between him and General Arnold! for
the latter was despised when living and execrated when
dead—and justly. Although he fought like a tiger in
battle, yet his courage partook more of the nature of a
reckless robber than a truly brave man. And as to treachery and meanness, he had no equal. When his innocent
coxswain and six bargemen vigorously plied the oar at his
bidding, and put him safely aboard the British ship, he
coolly turned round and gave them up as prisoners of
war! A fitting climax to his high treason! But when
the facts became known to Sir Henry Clinton, he ordered
the barge given up and the men released at once; and so
they manned the boat and returned to their kindred and
friends, in spite of the mean treachery of their late commander.

A romance has been thrown around the memory of
Maj. Andre, which seems to increase with the progress of
years; while the name of Arnold will stand conspicuous

to the end of time, as the only American officer of note who proved traitor to the glorious cause of his country.

Mrs. Arnold, on her arrival at her father's home in Philadelphia, was immediately warned by the Executive Council that she could not remain there. Although her father, herself and connections tried every means to have her remain, under a solemn pledge not to correspond with her husband; yet, so fully did the Council believe her equally guilty with her husband, that her request was firmly denied, and go she must. She was sent at once to her husband at New York city. She feared insult and injury on the way, but her fears were groundless. While the whole country resounded with execrations of her husband, and his effigy was dragged through village streets and burnt at the stake, or hung on a gallows, she passed the whole distance without injury or insult. Indeed, so scrupulous were the populace not to make war on a defenceless woman, that on her arriving at a village at nightfall, where they had prepared to burn her husband's effigy, they forebore, returned to their homes and left the wife or traitor to sleep in peace.

Once, only, she visited Philadelphia again, and that was about five years after her exile. And although the war was over and peace established, yet she was treated with such scorn and neglect, that her stay was short; she left in disgust, and declared she would never come there again. She was a woman of fine personal appearance, good education and many attractions, and tried hard to sustain a fair social position for herself and husband in England; but only with partial success; for her husband was generally " slighted and sometimes insulted." She died in London in the Winter of 1796.

I then said, the course he took in the French Revolution was an enigma to some of our people, for they did not distinctly understand what he would have done had he the power. He said, he supposed it might be so, especially to those not well versed in the events of the time; but he could readily explain it. He was not, under the circumstances, for a Republic. He thought the people of France were not in a condition to form a Republican government, or to sustain one if made; and after events showed that he was right in that opinion. He was for an improved and modified Monarchy. He did not wish to destroy, but to reform. Louis XVI. had many good qualities, but he lacked the needful firmness and energy for a successful ruler, especially for the times in which he lived. Marie Antoinette, the Queen, was spirited, firm and aristocratic. The King would seemingly yield everything; and the Queen, nothing. He found himself between two fires— the extreme Republicans disliked him because he advocated a constitutional monarchy; and the Court party, especially the Queen, did the same, in spite of the great services he had rendered them, because he advocated a reform. At length, the Extremists, led by Danton, Marat and Robespierre, ruled; imprisoned the King and Queen, forbade the army to obey his commands, and ordered his arrest. Satisfied that an arrest would be fatal; that he, like other prisoners, could have no fair trial, he felt compelled to quit France to save his life.

The beginning of the French Revolution may be said to have begun at the destruction of the Bastile on the 14th of August, 1789. The enthusiasm and power of the mob were so great, that this horrid citadel in Paris was captured in four hours, which was surrounded with seemingly impassable ditches, inaccessible towers, and ramparts covered with powerful artillery, and which had withstood, for twenty-three days, an army commanded by the great Conde. After its capture, it was demolished to its very foundations; and the key was sent by Lafayette to Gen. Washington, who put it into a glass case;

and probably it may be seen at Mount Vernon at the present day. Had lawless power ended with the destruction of the Bastile, all humane people would have been satisfied; but one might as well try to direct or control a tempest as a lawless mob.

On the 19th of August, 1792, he left his native land to seek an asylum for himself and family, until the "reign of terror" was over. At that time, he was at the head of the army, far away from Lagrange, and could not go there and live. But he had a hope, and even belief, that his wife and children would not be molested; but he did not then fully realize what the madness of lawless mobs might do.

He wished to come to America, but could not reach the sea-coast; his only course seemed to be, to flee to some neutral territory, and there find an asylum, or from whence he could embark for America. On reaching Rochefort in Netherlands, he found himself in the neighborhood of an Austrian army. He asked for a passport through the country, and found a prison. He was first imprisoned at Luxembourg, and then placed in a common cart and, closely guarded, was transported to Wessel, on the Rhine, within the Prussian dominions. Here he was imprisoned, with heavy manacles locked on his hands and feet.

Although he had kept up his courage, and determined to brave the worst, yet, at length, nature yielded in spite of all his efforts. The cold, damp air of his cell, added to the hardships he was compelled to endure, brought on sickness, which, for a time, precluded all hope of recovery. The hair all came off from his head, and he was reduced to a skeleton. In this deplorable condition, the King of Prussia said he could be released from prison, if he would assist in conquering France. He met the message with the scorn it merited; and bade the officer tell his master he was still LAFAYETTE.

The King, enraged at this, and annoyed at the great importunities from America and **Europe** for his release, determined to send him to a more gloomy abode, out of his dominion. The dungeons of Wessel were not dark and gloomy enough to suit the monarch's malignity; so, without warning, **he was** again hurried into a cart at night, and with the utmost secrecy, sent to the dungeon **at** Olmutz in Austria. Austria is always consistent **with** herself, and a fitting place for such a **horrid dungeon as** the fortress of Olmutz. While other nations have **im**proved, she has only "marked time," and still is a dark spot on the face of civilized Europe.

Olmutz is a city of 12,000 inhabitants, and a hundred and fifty miles from Vienna. The dungeon is on an island in the city, and is a relic of the dark ages. Its walls are of stone, twelve feet thick, and surrounded by a moat, more or less filled with water. Lafayette's cell had a door for entrance, and one window two feet square, with a grate outside and in. The wall was so thick that the sun never shone in his prison, nor could he see any outward objects. He always suffered from its dampness, **and in** the Winter severely by the cold.

As he entered **the cell it** was announced to him that he **never** could come out again alive, nor could he hold **any** communion with the outer **world, and that his** wife and children would never know where **he** was or what became of him. The jailers were prohibited **from** pronouncing his name, and all the prisoners must be referred to only by the number of their cells. And, under the pretence that such a state of confinement might induce suicide, he would not be accommodated with knives or forks.

The dimensions of his room were about 10 by 12 feet, **and the** furniture was an old table, broken chair, and a **sack** of mouldy straw. A scanty allowance of coarse **food** was brought him twice a day. Books were excluded, and he heard no human voice, except the gruff tones of the jailer.

After Lafayette's transfer to Olmutz, all knowledge of the place of his confinement was excluded and unknown to his friends. They believed him alive somewhere in Prussia or Austria, and tried hard to discover his dungeon. At length, after he had been imprisoned for three years—one at Wessel, and two at Olmutz,—a daring spirit assumed the task, both of finding where he was, and rescuing him if possible. This was Dr. Erick Bollman, a young German physician, who had just finished his education and obtained his degrees. Although he had never seen Lafayette, and was personally unacquainted with him, yet he was well posted in his public career, and a great admirer of his character. Not having sufficient funds of his own for the undertaking, after selling his books, he procured the needful amount of a banker in Hamburg. Leaving Hamburg, he assumed the character of a traveller in pursuit of knowledge. He soon learned that Lafayette had been transferred to Austria, and borne away to Olmutz. He then selected a place for a temporary retreat if successful, some twenty miles away, near the frontier, and then proceeded to Olmutz. He did not know for a certainty that Lafayette was then there, and could make no direct inquiry, for that would create suspicion and defeat all his plans. At length, he discovered that several State prisoners were confined in the citadel of Olmutz, and thought it probable that Lafayette was among the number. Acting on this supposition, Dr. Bollman visited the hospital in that city, and made the acquaintance of the first surgeon of that institution, presuming that he also visited the captives in prison. He could not, however, ask him anything about Lafayette; but obtained the knowledge he desired by indirect means.

The surgeon proved to be an upright and intelligent

man, **of** good sense and humane feelings. The acquaintance seemed to be mutually agreeable; **and** after several interviews the conversation turned on the effect **of** moral impressions **on** the constitution by imprisonment, when Dr. Bollman abruptly drew a pamphlet from his pocket and remarked : "Since we are on the subject, you attend the State prisoners at the Fortress, Lafayette among **the** number, and his health is much impaired. Show him **this** pamphlet, and tell him a traveller left it with you, **who** lately saw in London the persons named **in it,** and that they are as much attached to him as ever, and it will do him more good than all your drugs." Perceiving the surgeon **did not** know what to reply, he changed the subject and soon left him.

Calling at the hospital in a few days, the surgeon, of his own accord, said he had given his pamphlet to Gen. Lafayette, who was much pleased, and wished to know something more of one or two friends named in it. On this, the Doctor, appearing to have a blank piece of paper about him, but prepared for the emergency, for he had written **it** all over on one side with invisible ink, (lemon juice,) **sat down** and wrote a few lines on the other side in reply **to the** inquiries, and finished by saying, **"I am glad of the** opportunity **of** addressing you these words, which, *when read with your usual warmth*, will afford **to a heart** like yours some consolation." The italic words were a sufficient hint to the quick-minded Lafayette ; and by the heat of a lamp, made the words readable on the other side of the **paper.**

To avoid suspicion, Dr. Bollman quitted Olmutz the next day, visited Vienna and other places, and at length called on the surgeon at Olmutz, who then returned him **the** pamphlet. On examining it, he found the margin **had been** written over with invisible ink ; from which he learned that Lafayette, on account **of** feeble health, **was** permitted, on certain days, to take an airing in an open carriage, and that must be the time to release him, if at all. Dr. Bollman ascertained that Lafayette had a driver on the box of the carriage, an officer by his side and two soldiers standing up behind, all armed. Deeming that too formidable an array to attack alone, he went to Vienna to find at least one coadjutor. But where could he find a daring spirit like himself? Thus far, he had not dared to reveal his secret to any man; and to whom could he reveal it without an almost certainty of being betrayed?

In this dilemma, he visited the leading hotel in Vienna, and there saw and became acquainted with a young man, whom he found to be of uncommon talent, decision and enthusiasm. This was Col. Francis Kinlock Huger, of South Carolina, at whose father's house Lafayette first lodged when he came to America in 1777. Francis was then a mere child of three years, and all he remembered of Lafayette was, that he used to dandle him on his knee when at his father's house. His father, Maj. Benjamin Huger, was now dead, but his mother was still alive; and he, having come to his majority, was making the tour of Europe. Although he had but a slight recollection of Gen. Lafayette, yet he had heard him so much spoken of in his family, and so well posted up in his course in the Revolution, that he was ready to "do and dare" anything on his account. It seemed that he was providentially there at the time, for it is not probable that Dr. Bollman would have found any other reliable man who would have joined him in such a perilous attempt. Col. Huger at once entered into all his plans with enthusiastic zeal, and devoted himself to their execution.

Two good saddle horses were at once purchased, and a faithful groom to attend them. In this plight they entered Olmutz, and put up at a hotel as travellers. A relay of horses was obtained, and the groom took them to the place of rendezvous. On the 8th day of November, the carriage with Lafayette was seen emerging from the town gate, and the rescuers followed after. They were armed with pistols, but loaded only with powder, for they did not intend to take life, and were only to be used for intimidation. At two or three miles from the gate the carriage left the high road, and passed into a less inhabited tract and more open country. At length Lafayette's carriage stopped, and he and the officer got out to walk. The carriage, with the guard, drove on, but kept in sight. This was the time, no doubt, for the rescue; and galloping up, Dr. Bollman dismounted, seized the officer's sword, but before he could draw it from the scabbard, the officer seized it also, but still kept one hand hold of Lafayette. In the struggle all three came to the ground together. Dr. Bollman had the officer by the collar, and held him fast: Col. Huger then dismounted, released Lafayette, gave him a bag of gold, mounted him on his horse, and he was off and out of sight in a minute. When Lafayette was gone the strife ceased. The guard, instead of helping the officer, leaped from the carriage and ran the nearest route to the prison to give the alarm; and the officer, when released, did the same.

The rescuers, then, thought it was time to make their own escape; but they had but one horse. The calculation had been for both to ride the same horse, and both mounted. But, unfortunately, they had given Lafayette the one they designed for that purpose, and the other would not carry double, reared and threw them both off. Col. Huger then said: "This will never do. Gen. Lafayette wants you; mount the horse and be off, and I will take care of myself." Dr. Bollman soon reached the place of retreat, but Lafayette was not there! He could have escaped himself well enough, but would not, until he had ascertained what had become of General Lafayette. It seems, he had mistaken the direction, taken the wrong road, found no relays of horses, and rode some twenty miles until he had exhausted his horse as well as himself. The result was, that all three were separately, and unknown to each other, taken prisoners and put in separate prison cells. Gen. Lafayette was returned to his miserable dungeon again, put in irons, and still more harshly treated. Three short days only had he been permitted to breathe the pure air of heaven; and then, returned to his former dismal abode, with no hope that his sufferings would be ended except by death.

. Col. Huger was chained to the floor in a small arched dungeon, six by eight feet, without light, and with only bread and water for food; and once in six hours, by day and night, the guard would enter with a lantern, examine the walls and each link in his chains. To his earnest request to know what had become of Dr. Bollman and General Lafayette, he received no answer. To his still more earnest request, that he might send to his mother in America, merely the words, "*I am alive*," he received a rude refusal.

Dr. Bollman was also put in chains, and conducted to a dismal dungeon half under ground. Only a faint light came in through an oblique aperture made through a thick wall. Neither light nor books were allowed him, and his food was limited to what could be procured at four cents a day! The trial of Bollman and Huger was protracted during the whole Winter. The government proceeded with caution, for it was believed that others were in the plot, as it was not deemed hardly possible that two young men, unaided and alone, should, out of mere patriotic motives, attempt the rescue of one personally a stranger to them. At length, by the aid and strong efforts of Count Metrowsky, a nobleman living near the prison, and a friend of Dr. Bollman's family, after eight months' imprisonment, they were both released on two weeks' additional confinement. After their release, they left Austria at once, and just in time; for in a few hours after they had left Olmutz, orders came from Vienna for their re-arrest; and a second trial might have ended fatally. But they were out of Austria and out of the reach of the minions of arbitrary power.

Col. Huger, having had enough of his European tour, returned, at once, to gladden the heart of his mother in South Carolina. She hailed him as one risen from the dead, for she had given him up for lost.

In 1824, General Lafayette and Col. Huger accidentally met in the city of New York. Although they had not seen each other for thirty years, they both recognized each other at once, and had a cordial meeting. Col. Huger accompanied the General in his trip up the Hudson; and when they returned to New York city, they were obliged to part. Col. Huger was on his way to Boston on business; and General Lafayette, on his way to Washington City. The General regretted very much he could not return to Boston and introduce his attempted deliverer to his friends there. But he did the best he could; for he gave him a cordial letter of introduction to Mayor Quincy, and begged him to show him all kind attentions, the same as to himself; and the Mayor did it handsomely, for Col. Huger was greatly lionized during his visit.

It is not known, that Dr. Bollman and the General ever met after that eventful day of the rescue. In a few years, the Doctor came to America, became acquainted with Herman Blannerhassett, a countryman of his, on that paradise of an island bearing his name, in the Ohio river. There, Blannerhassett had built an elegant mansion house, and surrounded it with beautiful walks, gardens and flowers. But there, the cruel spoiler came, as

in blessed Eden of old, and induced him to leave all to
destruction, and join Col. Burr in an expedition down
the Ohio and Mississippi rivers, to colonize lands in Mexico, or treason against the United States, whichever it
might be. Col. Aaron Burr and Blannerhassett were
arrested for treason, and acquitted. Dr. Bollman joined
his friend in the expedition, but it does not appear that
any crime was alleged against him. He then proceeded
to England, and became an eminent physician in London,
published a treatise on banking and another on hygiene,
and died there in 1821. General Lafayette met two of
Dr. Bollman's daughters in Philadelphia in 1824, when
on his way to Washington City.

The Blannerhassett Island comprises an area of some
180 acres; is beautiful by nature, and had been much improved by art. Here the proprietor and his accomplished
wife and interesting children resided in quiet happiness
and peace. When the spoiler came and seduced him from
his secluded retreat, an Ohio mob invaded the premises,
burnt the buildings, destroyed all the improvements, and
laid waste the whole island. He never returned to the
island again, but after his acquittal went to his native land
in Europe, and died there broken hearted. Who owns
the island now, or the condition it is in, I have no means
of knowing.

The reason why the mob invaded the island was because
they believed Col. Burr was plotting treason, and preparing to make war on the United States, and as Blannerhassett was associated with him, he was found in bad
company, and had to suffer the consequences, guilty or
not.

It seems to us strange, that the rescue of Lafayette, so
sagaciously planned and promptly executed, should be
productive of such sad results. It may well be asked,
why General Lafayette, an invalid as he was, should be

sent off alone, through a strange country, with only slight directions, hastily given. Had it been successful, it would have saved two years of agony that cannot be imagined, much less described. His fetters were so closely fastened to his ancles as to cause great pain; the iron band around his waist had a chain attached to it, and fastened to the wall; but so short, that he could not comfortably lie down. No light or fire was permitted in his cell, and he was denied suitable food or decent clothes. In the severe Winter of 1795, he suffered severely from cold, and became miserably emaciated. And to add to his bodily sufferings, mental anxieties were added. He was made to believe that he was only reserved for public execution, and that his chivalrous deliverers had already perished on the scaffold. Nor was he permitted to know whether his family were yet alive, or had fallen under the revolutionary axe.

But the failure of the rescue was not all evil. It gave his friends and his wife a clue to his place of confinement and the condition he was in. After her husband had been imprisoned, she herself was arrested and sent to her husband's estates in the South of France, 320 miles from Paris, and there kept as a State prisoner for more than a year. When her husband's estates were confiscated, as well as her own, she was brought to Paris and there imprisoned. By the unwearied exertions of Washington and our minister at Paris, she was released, and at liberty to go whither she would. She might have come to America, as she was cordially invited to do; but, just at this time, the news of the attempted rescue of her husband reached her ears; and that settled at once the course she should pursue. Sending her son, George Washington, to George Cabot of Boston, to be by him sent to Mount Vernon, she procured passports from the American Minister at Paris for herself and two daughters, and started

11

for Vienna. She had then three children—two daughters and one son. Anastasia was 16, Virginia 13, and George Washington 11. The first-born daughter, Henrietta, died in childhood, when her father was in the revolutionary war.

On her arrival at Vienna, the Emperor, Francis I., received her coldly ; but after earnest importunity, her request to visit her husband was granted,·but with such conditions that he supposed she would not accept them. They were, that she should carry nothing with her for the comfort of her husband, and never be permitted to come out of the prison while she lived. Harsh and barbarous as the terms were, she accepted them at once, and she and her two daughters entered the prison. The meeting cannot be described by words ; hardly imagined ! The prison walls rung with a joy that had never echoed there before ! For three long and grevious years, he had not heard the least news of his family ; and there his beloved wife and two daughters stood before him ! Separate apartments were assigned the daughters, each one to her solitary room ; and only eight hours in the twenty-four were they allowed to be with their parents ; and then they were constantly annoyed by the visits of the keeper, under the plea that they might be plotting mischief.

The imprisonment of the daughters, in its details, partook more of the nature of satanic malevolence than anything else. They had committed no crime ; were neither accused nor suspected of any ; and yet, their confinement was made to be needlessly irksome and oppressive. But eight hours in the twenty-four were they allowed to be with their parents ; and the other sixteen, were confined in separate rooms, and not allowed to be company for each other !

After an imprisonment for more than a year, the emaciation and feebleness of Madame Lafayette were so great, that her husband urged her to ask leave to go into more healthy quarters for a time, to recruit her health. **She** did; and what was the answer? **Such as** a despot might give. She and her daughters **might leave** the prison as soon as they pleased, but never to return there again, and immediately quit the kingdom. Harsh as the terms were, her husband urged her to accept them for the sake of her children as well as herself. But she turned to him at once and firmly said: "**My** dear husband, **I** had rather *die* with you here in prison, than *live* at the beautiful **La-grange without you.**" He urged her no more, and came to the conclusion that they all were destined to die there together!

But Providence **had determined that Lafayette** and his wife and daughters should **not** perish within the prison walls of Olmutz. Austria might well spurn the entreat-ies of America and England, and frown at the words of reproach echoed over the continent; yet she quailed un-der the stern mandates of Napoleon. The commands of the "Conqueror of Italy" must be obeyed, and Lafayette and his family were set free. On the 23d of September, 1797, Lafayette, after an imprisonment of over five years, and his wife and daughters, after a confinement with him **for twenty-two** months, were permitted once more to **see the light of day, and** breathe the pure air of heaven. And all these enormities and afflictions were endured without judgment of law, or even the accusation of crime!

But there must have been a *cause* for his imprisonment, and what was it? Simply this: He was a decided be-liever in, and **a** powerful advocate for, rational liberty and freedom; and that kings should not possess arbitrary power, but be subject to laws, as well as their subjects. When he was first arrested and imprisoned, the joyous tid-ings were sent to the crowned heads of Europe, and caused a jubilee among all advocates of arbitary power. They **hardly dared** kill him by a public execution, but to kill him in such a manner that none should know, outside of prison walls, what became of him.

The motives of Napoleon in liberating Lafayette are not distinctly known, for he had not caused his name to be stricken from the "proscribed list," and he could not return to France. He, therefore, sought a retreat on neutral ground, and went to Holstein, a dependency of Denmark; and at the little town of Welmoldt he enjoyed rest and repose. Little George was sent for, and the family were once more all together. But his patrimony, as well as that of his wife, had been confiscated, and he was destitute of the comforts of life. In this emergency, two English ladies, in token of their deep sympathy, sent him four thousand pounds, which fully relieved him of all his immediate wants. The names of these benevolent ladies are not known. The banker who sent the money was not at liberty to disclose their names, so that the General never knew who his benefactors were.

In the latter part of the year 1799, the Directory was overthrown and the Consulate established, with the victorious Napoleon at its head. When this was known to Lafayette, he went to Paris and demanded of Napoleon his rights as a citizen. His demand was tacitly granted, his name was stricken from the "proscribed list," and Lagrange restored to his wife; but his large estates in the South of France were never restored to him. To the beautiful estate of Lagrange, situated 40 miles East of Paris, consisting of a thousand acres of productive land, on which is an ancient castle of ample dimensions, Gen. Lafayette brought his family, and they were all together again on their native soil. And at this delightful retreat the family lived the remainder of their days. A secluded life the General lived, during the whole of Napoleon's reign; although urged at times to take high office in his government.

On the 24th of December, 1807, died the devoted wife,
Madame Lafayette. Although not unexpected, yet it was
a shock the family could not bear with composure; and
when she gave them her last smile, bathed her death-bed
in tears. She lived ten years after her release from the
prison of Olmutz, but never fully recovered her previous
health. Her maiden name was Anastasia de Noailles,
and daughter of the Duke de Ayen. Her married life was
thirty-four years, and she was forty-seven years old at the
time of her death. Her life is one of the brightest in the
annals of female heroism, conspicuous alike for her public charities and domestic virtues.

In 1814 passed another act in the great drama of
French politics. Napoleon was dethroned, sent to Elba,
and Louis XVIII. was seated on the throne of his fathers.
In eleven months Napoleon appeared on the stage again,
dethroned the king, and occupied his place. After the
battle of Waterloo, Napoleon was deposed, and the king,
by the power of his allies, was restored to his throne
again. In all these changes Lafayette took no active part.
He called once on the king, was decently treated, but
never called again. From 1818 to 1824 he had been
elected, and sat in the Chamber of Deputies; but in the
last named year, the king put forth all his power and de-
feated his election. He thought that was a favorable time
to visit his friends in America, which he had for a long
time contemplated to do. And his son George was very
anxious to visit a country he had heard so much of, and
seen so little, and that little was in early youth. His
secretary and son were taking notes of the trip through
the country, and on their return to France, would be
looked over, and if anything could be made out of them
worthy of publication, and were printed in his lifetime, I
should have a copy.

Let it not be supposed that the narrative of Gen. Lafayette's imprisonment and attempted rescue was mainly derived from him. On all other subjects he was free to converse, but on this his voice faltered, and he became silent; tears were on his face, and I perceived that the remembrance of his sufferings was too painful, and changed the subject. But most of the facts are obtained from an account given by Dr. Bollman himself, and published in a magazine soon after the event.

Nor, let it be supposed that his friends were inactive and silent during all his long imprisonment. General Washington, then President of the United States, did all he could in his official capacity, as well as a private citizen, to relieve him from his loathsome dungeon. A number of leading papers in London and Hamburg published a series of articles exposing in sarcastic and cutting language the infamous conduct of Prussia and Austria, to the scorn of all Europe.⸸ Their perfidy in detaining a prisoner, contrary to the rights of nations and humanity, was condemned with such eloquence and scathing criticism that the tyrants were goaded to speak in their own defence. And what did they say? Only this: That the *freedom* of Gen. Lafayette was incompatible with the safety of the present governments of Europe! And this was their only apology for their inquisitorial cruelties to him.

Two attempts were made in the British Parliament to liberate Gen. Lafayette—one on the 17th of March, 1794, and the other on the 16th of December, 1796. At the latter date, Gen. Fitzpatrick, after a feeling and eloquent introduction, introduced a resolution into the House of Commons requesting the King to intercede, in such a manner as he deemed proper, for the deliverance of Gen. Lafayette and the other State prisoners. He was supported by Col. Tarlton, who had fought against Lafayette in Virginia, during our revolution; and by Fox, Wilberforce, Sheridan, and Greg; and opposed by Pitt, Burke,

Windham and Dundas. Fox, in particular, pleaded the cause of Lafayette in one of the most impassioned speeches he ever made ; but all, all in vain ! The motion was lost by the large majority of 132 against 32.

On the Journal of the Congress of the United States of. the 3d of March, 1797, will be found a record which will stand through all time, as a dark spot in the annals of our country. It is some relief, however, to know that it was as odious to the *citizens* of the country then as it is to the present generation.

On that day, the orator and and Statesman, Robert Goodloe Harper, introduced a resolution into the House of Representatives, requesting the President to take such measures as he might deem expedient to adopt, to restore to liberty our fellow-citizen, Gen. Lafayette.

Nothithstanding this resolution was advocated with the glowing eloquence of a Harper, it was rejected by a yea and nay vote of 52 to 32 ! This result, no doubt, may be attributed to the cold, calculating fear of foreign entanglements and disputes ; and, therefore, the gallant Lafayette, who had spent his time and substance, and perilled his life in the cause of our independence, must be left to the tender mercies of a tyrant, with a fair prospect of perishing in a loathesome dungeon ! But, thanks to God, the stern mandates of Napoleon effected what neither the British Parliament nor the American Congress dared to attempt !   .

General Lafayette was born on the 6th of September, 1757, in the province of Auvergne, which is in the central part of the Southern division of France, and three hundred and twenty miles South of Paris. The estate consisted of five thousand acres of land, surrounded by mountains in the distance, and presents the most delightful scenery to be found in France. The ancestral Chateau de Chavagnae, where he was born, was built in 1701, on the site of a more ancient one destroyed by fire. It stands amid an amphitheatre of mountains, commanding a magnificent view of encircling mountain summits. Interesting as the birthplace of Lafayette may be, it contains, at this day, hardly any memorials of himself. Even the room in which he was born is not known; and a single portrait of him, taken in his boyhood, is the only evidence of his early residence there.

He belonged to one of the most ancient and noble families of France. The family, from time immemorial, was noted for ability, patriotism and integrity; so that the name of Lafayette was but another name for integrity and honor. His father was a Colonel in the French army, and killed in the battle of Minden, a few months before he was born. The care of his infancy and youth was left, therefore, entirely to his mother, who was a woman of education, excellent qualities and rare attainments.

He entered college in Paris at the early age of 12; was fond of books, and obtained a good classical as well as military education. His love of books continued through life, and was a great source of enjoyment in his leisure hours.

In 1770, at the age of 14, his mother died; and as he was an only child, he was left sole heir to a large estate; and, although surrounded by parasites and flatterers, never indulged in dissipation, but applied his great income to some useful purpose, rather than spending it in riotous living, as young men often do.

In April, 1774, he was married, at the early age of 17, to the Countess Anastasie de Noailles, daughter of the Duke d'Ayen, and brought to his own a heart full of virtue, courage and conjugal affection, as well as large estates; although she, herself, was the greatest treasure of all. Her estates, together with his own, gave him a revenue of more than $37,000 a year.

He became a great favorite at Court, especially with the brilliant but aristocratic Queen, Marie Antoinette, who, in after life, when he advocated reform, turned against him with the unforgiving and relentless ferocity of an enraged woman. She was an Austrian Princess; and as her cousin was on the throne at the time of Lafayette's imprisonment at Olmutz, her influence, dead or alive, no doubt followed him there, and caused his extremest sufferings.

General Lafayette was a precocious youth; or, rather, seemed to have no youth at all, for he appeared to leap from childhood to manhood at a bound; and while others of his own age were at school, he had obtained his own education, and was in the battle field, bravely contending for the rights of man.

General Lafayette would be deemed a man of note among thousands. He was nearly six feet in height, broad-shouldered, robust, rather inclined to corpulency; full and florid face, light complexion, and large, full and expressive eyes. He had great power of face; and the muscles of his forehead and face would readily move, and instantly change "from grave to gay, from lively to severe." His perceptions were very acute; and he would readily adapt himself to all persons, times and occasions. On his last visit here, he had been a widower eighteen years: and when he took leave of President Adams at Washington, Sept. 6, 1825, it was on the anniversary of his birthday; and he was exactly sixty-eight years of age. He spoke the English language very well, but slower than a native American. He said when he left this country in 1784, he could speak English quite fluently; but being 40 years out of practice, it took time to express his thoughts in that language.

General Lafayette lived nine years and eight months after he left this country in 1825, very much at his ease,

12

highly respected, and often a member of the Chamber of
Deputies. At the beautiful Lagrange, surrounded by his
family and friends, full of honors, at peace with himself
and all the world, he went to his rest May 20, 1834, aged
seventy-six years and eight months—the last surviving
Major-General of the revolutionary war.

"He sleeps his last sleep; he's fought his last battle;
No sounds can awake him to glory again."

His death caused a great sensation in Europe, as well
as in America, and due honors were paid to his memory.
He was buried in a small cemetery near Paris, by the side
of his wife; and in a few years his son, George Washington Lafayette, was laid there also. Now, all his children are dead, and there buried; but numerous grand-
children, and great-grandchildren, inhabit the beautiful
Lagrange.

It must be admitted, however, that Gen. Lafayette was
a most remarkable man. So varied were the incidents of
his life, and so momentous the affairs of the world at the
time he lived, that his character cannot be delineated in a
sentence. Let us allude to a few prominent incidents in
his life :—

In the first place, he was a kind, humane and benevolent man. In 1787, a fire occurred on Beach street, Boston, which destroyed one hundred buildings, sixty of which
were dwelling houses of people in moderate circumstances.
When the news reached France, the General sent $1500 to
Samuel Beck, to be distributed among the sufferers. In
1778, he rescued a British Captain, about to be executed
by Gen. Arnold. Near the American camp he found a
soldier, meanly clad, sitting at the foot of a tree, with his
elbows on his knees and his hands up to his face in deep
melancholy. On inquiring the cause of his grief, the soldier said, he had lately enlisted, but that he was so sadly
poor that he had left his wife and two children at home

entirely destitute. The General at once relieved the family and clothed the soldier. An Irishman, who had published a newspaper in Ireland of liberal principles, had to flee his country, and came to Philadelphia. He needed $400 to establish a paper there. The General gave him the sum, and he established his paper and became a patriotic and useful citizen. On taking leave of Capt. Allyn, of the ship Cadmus, he made valuable presents to all the officers and crew.

In 1786, he wrote to Gen. Washington to assist him in devising a plan to elevate the African race. He says, "Let us unite in purchasing a small estate, where we may try the experiment to free the negroes and employ them only as tenants." But, impatient of delay, he tried the experiment alone, by purchasing an estate at Cayenne, in South American waters, with all the negroes upon it; freed them, and had the pleasure of finding his plan successful. In this, he had the cordial sympathy of Washington, Adams, Franklin, Jefferson, Madison, Patrick Henry, and others. Washington wrote to him, under date of May 10, 1786, "Your late purchase in Cayenne, with a view of emancipating your slaves, is a generous and noble proof of your humanity. Would to God a like spirit might diffuse itself generally into the minds of the people of this country." We have already alluded to his contributing one hundred and forty thousand dollars of his own funds to the cause of American Independence, besides giving arms and uniforms to the Continental army. But why pursue this subject further? His whole life was characterized by kind acts, considerate charities and noble deeds. Turn we, then, to some of the tokens of regard bestowed upon him :

In the time of the Revolution, Congress presented him an elegant sword ; and a similar one was presented him at New York in 1824, by the Ninth Regiment of Artillery.

Dr. Franklin's cane was presented to him at Philadelphia, and at Bergen, N. J., he was presented with a gold-headed cane, made out of an apple tree that shaded Washington and Lafayette in 1779. At Mount Vernon, he was presented by Mr. Custis with a ring, containing Gen. Washington's hair, and his Masonic sash and jewels. At Baltimore, he was presented with an elegant carriage by the makers, and he took it with him on his trip through the Southern States in 1825. But I turn to things more etherial and sublime. He has been complimented and honored with innumerable speeches, addresses and letters; with the deep-toned voices of cannon and bells, the cheers of musical bands, and the shouts of welcome from millions of people, all combined in one harmonious strain, echoing from the great lakes to the greater gulf, and from the Atlantic ocean to the great rivers and mountains of the West. And his name will live—live, not only in the hearts of a grateful people, but in the names of mountains, forts, counties, towns, corporations and societies, as well as in the names of children and children's children to the latest generation.

The degree of Doctor of Laws was conferred upon him by many colleges; the right of citizenship, by the United States; and the freedom of States and cities was granted to him and his posterity. But to show he was not ambitious of worldly honors, it should be stated that many of the high offices and honors he declined. In the French revolution, he refused to be made King; and afterwards, when he was strongly urged to become President of a French Republic, he firmly declined. He was, also, tendered high offices by Napoleon, but declined them all.

In 1803, he was appointed Governor of Louisiana, by President Jefferson, and urged to accept it; but he respectfully but firmly declined the high honor.

And to show his disinterested patriotism, it is only

needful to state that he refused to receive any compensation for all his services and expenditures in both the French and American revolutions. When urged by the French government to receive some compensation for all his great services, he replied that "his fortune had been sufficient to place him above want, and had sufficed for two revolutions; and if a third should occur, for the benefit of the people, the whole should be devoted to it."

In addition to all this, and to show he was a man of uncommon liberality, it should be stated that Congress, in 1803, granted him 11,000 acres of land, to be located in the newly acquired territory of Louisiana. His agent located a thousand acres adjoining the city of New Orleans. In 1807, Congress, seemingly unconscious of this location, granted to the city of New Orleans a large portion of the very land entered by General Lafayette. When informed of the fact, and that his title was unquestionable, and the value of the land was from fifty to a hundred thousand dollars, he wrote to his agent that he would not consent to inquire into the validity of his title; for he could not think of entering into a litigation with any public body in the United States; and gave positive instructions to his agent to relinquish his entry, and make a location elsewhere. He did so, and the new location proved of little value; but the land relinquished is an important part of the city of New Orleans, and worth millions.

I have said that General Lafayette was not only needful, but essential, to the success of our revolution. And now, in addition to all other considerations, I will state an important reason in confirmation of this. It is a well known fact, that it is difficult to make armies of different nations, even when engaged in the same cause, to act harmoniously together. This was often painfully witnessed in our revolution; and no one but General Lafayette could successfully negotiate between them and induce them to act efficiently together. This, at times, was an arduous task, and taxed his utmost powers. His great exertions were never more conspicuous and essential than in the case of Count D'Estang at Newport, and Count De Grasse at Yorktown.

General Lafayette was a man of great firmness and personal courage. He stood for the right against all odds, and never deserted a friend. This was fully exemplified in his joining the American revolution at the time he did; and when other hearts quailed he stood firm. His personal firmness was conspicuous, when he rode up to quiet and disperse a mob in the French revolution. The first salutation he got, was a musket shot. He felt the ball whistle by his ear; he changed not his position, but stretched himself up in the saddle, looked sternly at the quarter from whence the shot came, and firmly said: "Bring forth the assassin!" Straightway the mob fell upon the assassin and cut him to pieces; then shouted loud and repeated cheers for Lafayette, and at once dispersed.

Another instance of firmness and courage, that surpasses all ordinary comprehension, occurred at the prison of Olmutz. When the Austrian ministers found they must relinquish their prey, although unknown to Lafayette at the time, they attempted to compel him to receive his freedom on prescribed conditions; but he distinctly and firmly said, " he would perish within the prison walls, or leave them a free man."

He seems to have had a charmed life, for he passed through perils of shipwreck and mutiny on the ocean, the perils of a snagged boat on the great Western river; and faced many a hard fought battle in Europe and America, and escaped all these perils with merely a slight flesh wound on his person. He was more "the man of destiny" than Napoleon himself, and, like Marshal Ney, was "the bravest of the brave."

A sketch of Gen. Lafayette would be incomplete without a glance at the beautiful Lagrange and its occupants. The castle lies in the fertile district of La Brie, forty miles East of Paris, remote from any thoroughfare, and surrounded by forests. A more sequestered spot, distant from the bustling world, can hardly be imagined. Here are prolific orchards, cultivated fields, pleasant walks and antiquated woods. The castle is quadrangular in shape, with a round pointed tower at each angle. The building is ancient, and simply furnished. The wood is divided into beautiful lanes, intersecting with each other, and admirably adapted to solitary walks, or reading, in the dense shade.

The estate is divided into grass lands and cultivated fields, and dotted here and there with cottage buildings, but no fences. Here may be seen, in their season, orchards of fruit, fields of grain and meadows of grass.

Here, the General lived in rural simplicity and unostentatious hospitality; and few indeed are the Americans who did not pay their respects to the benefactor of their country. No idle ceremony awaited them; but, simply, a hearty welcome. His breakfast hour was eleven, but the children were served with a morning lunch, and dinner at five—two meals a day. After breakfast came the morning walk, starting all together, but soon separating into different parties, as inclination dictated. Sometimes the General, with his grandson, inspected his farm, his sheep-folds and cattle-stalls; looked over the peasantry at work, and had a cheerful word for all. Once a week, the peasantry assembled in an ample room in the castle in winter; and in summer, on the lawn, and danced to the merry sound of the violin. In this, the younger portion of the family joined. In the course of the evening an ample lunch was served to them all. The simplicity in dress of the whole family was remarkable. No finery was seen on any of them, and few ornaments. The General, himself, in youthful days, when ruffled shirts and ruffled wristers were fashionable, would have none of them. Should it be asked, how he could have enjoyed the gorgeous displays in this country, so lavishly exhibited, the answer is plain. He did like splendid scenes and rich ornaments, but not on his person. When a little school girl, in Boston, slipped a crown of laurels, interwoven with flowers, on his head, it came off quicker than it was put on, and placed on the seat beside him. When a like attempt was made at Yorktown, his quick hand caught the wreath and handed it to another. What man of observation was there here, who did not observe that the General, his son, and secretary, passed all over the country in the simplest garb imaginable, without any display of ornaments on dress. A writer, who visited Lagrange when the family were all alive and together, says: "Simple in dress as in the manner of living; it would be in vain to seek for splendid dresses, jewels, or any of the trappings of worldly vanity at Lagrange. The jewels of the Lafayette family are those of the mother of the Gracchi." Cannot *pious* American ladies take note of this?

Gen. Lafayette's private apartments consisted of two rooms, on the second floor. His bed room was a fair sized room, with a fire-place, and windows looking out on the lawn and woods in the rear of the castle. From this room, a door opened into his library, which was large, and in the turret, and nearly round. It is adorned with the busts of Washington, Franklin, and other distinguished Americans. By a window, is his desk, where he, with a spy-glass, could see on his left his whole farm and his stables; on his right, the park and an elegant lawn, covered with luxuriant grass; and also see his peasants at work, and enjoy the extensive scene before him. Here he kept his farm books, in which are registered a record of his crops and improvements, in his own hand.

Gen. Lafayette had a room in his castle, set apart as a kind of museum, which he called "America," in which were deposited his American gifts, curiosities, newspapers, pamphlets, &c., among which was seen, in a conspicuous place, Dr. Franklin's original printing press.

In a thorough investigation of the character of Gen. Lafayette, I had come to the conclusion that he was a most noble and perfect man ; and I could say, like Pilate of old, "I find no fault in him;" when I was taken all aback at my stupidity. Two writers, of some note, have discovered a most grievous fault, and it would seem he has most grievously answered it in another world! One says, "he finds no evidences of a Christian faith on his dying bed ; without which, all other virtues are dim and powerless in such an hour." And the other says, "If, to the noble qualities he possessed, had been added the pure faith and sublime hopes of the gospel, nothing would have been wanting to complete the portraiture of a perfect man." "Evidences and hopes!" and to whom given, to God or to man? Who presumes to be the vicegerent of the Almighty, and poke his nose into a death-bed scene, and pronounce judgment on a dying man?

When or where did Lafayette act or speak a word against the Christian religion? On the contrary, it is well known that he was no bigot, but for the largest religious liberty. Although educated as a Catholic, when the Protestants in the South of France complained of infringements on their religious rights, he hastened to that region, carefully investigated all their complaints, and had them redressed. Contrary to all rules of law or justice, these bigots call *no* evidence, the *strongest* evidence, and condemn accordingly.

13

And has it come to this, that when a remorseless murderer appears on the scaffold with his priest, and exhibits some sniveling signs of repentance, proclaims his peace made with God and sins forgiven, is endorsed as a saint and sent joyfully to Heaven; and a man who has spent a long life in doing all the good he could, but is not sagacious enough to have a priest, or pious deacon, at his dying bed; and, in his presence and hearing, *manifest* his Christian faith and hope, is denounced an infidel and sent to perdition!

I had supposed that religion was a private matter between man and his Maker, and not between man and man; and all outside human interference, arrogant impertinence. Where do these religionists get the doctrine that dying confessions take precedence of a long life of "good works?" The Bible says, "by their fruits ye shall know them!" And by this doctrine I stand, and doubt not in the company of all real Christians throughout the world. It is time that these criticisms on death-bed scenes should be treated with the contempt they deserve.

To cast a shade over the brightest characters cannot, surely, be a desirable employment for an honest, liberal mind; yet some men, of narrow minds and strong prejudices, undertake this insidious task, pursue it with a zeal that never tires, and authoritatively condemn without a particle of evidence whatever.

George Washington Lafayette, the General's only son, was so completely eclipsed by his father, that little is said or known of him. In most of the published accounts of the General's visits, his name is seldom mentioned at all; and yet, he was much of a gentleman, of good personal appearance, and well educated. Although he seemed reconciled to his position, yet it must have been rather unpleasant to him to pass through the country under such a dense shadow as hardly to be seen or recognized, amid the splendid scenes that surrounded him. He could not join in the shouts of welcome to his own father, and must have been often a mere silent looker-on. It must have been some relief, however, to see his father so highly honored, to whom he seemed to be much devoted. He had great fears that his father's strength was overtaxed, his constitution would be impaired, and, after the excitement was over, would linger and die.

When I took my seat in the stage coach at Pembroke, I sat by his side; and as neither of us cared to pay much attention to the passing events, we had, during two or three hours, an interesting conversation. He spoke the English language very well; I thought, more fluently than his father; and when I marvelled at this, he said he learned it in his early youth. That when his mother and two sisters went to seek his father at Olmutz, he was sent to Mount Vernon, staid there more than two years, studied the English language, and spoke it daily in common conversation. He formed a strong attachment for General Washington and his wife, and did not wonder that his father so highly esteemed them. Although he was kindly treated, and generally enjoyed himself very well, yet he had some very sad hours. He understood that his mother and sisters were in the prison at Olmutz with his father; but during all the time he was at Mount Vernon, he could not learn anything more, notwithstanding the great exertions of General Washington. He could not know whether they were alive or dead, sick or well; and the suspense, at times, was very severe. He did not let the General and Mrs. Washington know how sad he was, because it would have distressed them on his account, without the power of relieving. At length, the joyful tidings came, that his father, mother and sisters were all alive and out of prison, and he was sent for to join them at Welmbold in Denmark. He leaped for joy, ran out into the fields to shake off his exuberant feelings, that were too oppressive to hold. With all expedition, he embarked, and met them at last. The meeting was very affecting, mingled with joys and sorrows. They found him increased in size and a healthy boy; but he found them mere skeletons of what they were; and they appeared prematurely old. They attempted to tell him of the horrors of Olmutz, but could not. In time, they improved in health, were restored to Lagrange, and were quite happy.

The year before, he had gone with his father to visit Mount Vernon, and looked over the buildings and grounds. They were not in such complete order as in the days of Washington. They entered the tomb of Washington, paid their devoirs at his shrine, and wept full sore as they left. His stay was short; shorter than it would have been had he been alone; for his father was exceeding sorrowful, often in tears, and he urged an early departure.

Our conversation then turned upon the incidents of their tour through the country; and I perceived at once that he had been an attentive observer. He said, America was a rough looking country compared to France, but very interesting in scenery. Nature had done her work here on a large scale, and the mountains and rivers were wonders. It was something marvellous that they had travelled so many thousand miles, over hills and rough roads in stage coaches, and in steamers on the mighty rivers, and had not been in peril of life or limb but once; and that was in a steamer on the Mississippi river, when the boat was snagged. The snag was a big tree and pierced the boat entirely through, and came out above the upper deck, so that the boat sank in a few minutes. But another steamboat was at hand, and they were rescued, with the loss of his father's hat, a trunk containing a part of his correspondence, and the beautiful carriage presented to him at Baltimore. A hatter at Louisburg supplied him with a new hat, but his correspondence and carriage could not be restored.

We also discussed the political affairs of his country and mine; and the English and French languages. I said, that the French language was so full of silent letters, and words of different signification were pronounced so much alike, that it was difficult for a foreigner to speak or understand it. He said, that might be so, but the English language was under the same condemnation; much more, probably, than I was aware of. Now, *d-a* spells *day;* but you must needs add a useless *y;* and this applies to a large class of words. And why does *ditch* need a *t* more than *rich?* And how can a foreigner distinguish the difference in pronunciation between *ship* and *sheep?* I gave in.

He was of medium size, darker complexion than his father, and about forty years old when here. He served in the army of Napoleon from 1800 to the peace of Tilsit; was a brave and efficient warrior, and twice saved the life of his commander, General Grouchy; was his aid through all the hard-fought battles, and was recommended by him for promotion. But Napoleon would not promote a Lafayette, and struck his name from the list. In 1803, he married the daughter of Senator Tracy, a very accomplished lady. They had five children, and the eldest daughter was a great favorite of General Lafayette.

Anastasia, the eldest surviving daughter of the General, married Charles de Latour Maubourg; Virginia married M. de Lasterie, who bravely fought with his brother-in-law, George Washington Lafayette, in many battles: but being connected with the Lafayette family, obtained no promotion. General Lafayette's youngest child was a daughter, named Carolina, after a State—or, rather, two States—of the Union. She was the only child born after the return of Lafayette to Lagrange.

In conclusion, permit me to suggest the propriety of erecting a monument at the State capital, in commemoration of the noble deeds of General Lafayette. Monuments have been built, and great honors bestowed on successful generals, many of whom fought to enslave and oppress mankind, and were a curse to the age in which they lived. But a greater Patriot, Statesman and Warrior is here, whose voice, pen, sword and fortune were vigorously and liberally employed in vindication of the rights of man, and the freedom of his race. A large debt of gratitude we owe him, for the manifold blessings we now enjoy.

Should it be said, that, as he fought for the *whole* country, and was the Nation's Guest, a monument at the Capital in Washington City would be more appropriate, the answer must be, that he was the Guest of New Hampshire also, one of the original States for which he fought. And, moreover, the case seems to be resolved into this: a New Hampshire monument, or none at all. If any one doubts this, let him look at the long unfinished monument of Washington, at the Capital of the nation.

And will the State of New Hampshire ever enter into such an enterprise as this? Let it never be asked; but let the people en masse erect it. After plans have been made, and the cost ascertained, let subscription books be sent to every town in the State, subscriptions limited to one dollar each; and when the needful amount is obtained, let an agent of each town meet at Concord, and appoint all needful committees for the building of the monument. Let the subscription books be deposited in the archives of the State, so that the autographs of the donors will live in all time to come; and they will feel that they have contributed their mite to a most noble object, and immortalized their names. And so great will be the desire to see the autographs of the donors, that a fac-simile will be lithographed, published in a book, and handed down as an heir-loom to the latest posterity.

And now, permit me to make some suggestions in regard to its size and location. The high ground directly in the rear of the State House would seem to be the most fitting place for its location. If buildings are in the way, let them be purchased, and removed. Let there be ample space to fit up a beautiful lot, with a fountain, seats and shade trees. As to its shape and size, let it be an obelisk, similar to that on Bunker Hill; only let it be made of rubble, or rough hewed granite, laid in cement; and let it be of sufficient height to over-top all spires and build-ings—sharp set against the sky, with no other back-ground but the blue heavens. And then, let it be crowned with a statue of Gen. Lafayette, of colossal or heroic size, facing the East and the State House.

A small, polished shaft is suitable for an individual grave, or family tomb; but not appropriate for a public monument. That, like a rugged mountain in the land-scape, should only be seen in the distance. Nature has smooth buttercups and flowers, but majestic trees are rug-ged and rough.

And when the congregated wisdom of the State assem-ble at the capitol, and ambitious political partisans so far forget themselves as to "give up to party what was meant for manhood," enter into a personal debate, and bandy words that are neither decent nor true, let them take a recess, repair to "Monument Square," and cool off. Let them sit in the dense shade, drink of the cool fountain, read the inscriptions on the monument, and look aloft on the benign face of the image it bears; and hardened sin-ners indeed they must be who do not return to the State House wiser Legislators and better men. But, if any narrow minded partisan should be impervious to all influ-ences like these, he must be too insignificant to be seen with the naked eye, and become the shadowy shadow of a shade !

And now, as we are on the subject of Legislators, let us express the wish, or hope, that they may in the future, as in former days, be "diligent in business," and economical in expenditures; and never indulge in "talking against time," or charging the State for seven days' labor in a week, for only three days' work actually performed.

The statue of Lafayette will stand as the sentinel on a watch-tower, the guardian-angel of the city of Concord; and its benign influence will be felt. Its citizens will honor the name they bear, and *concord* and not *discord* will be known, seen and felt throughout all its borders, and the State will justly be proud of its capital.

Concord has now many prominent features that are an honor to the city and State. Its reformatory and sanitary institutions, state house, halls, churches, stores and hotels are of the first order; and yet the Lafayette monument, when built, will be the most attractive feature of the city; save only the asylum for the insane. That stands on such a delightful eminence, commanding such a splendid view of the city and surrounding country, that it is a most attractive retreat for the sane as well as the insane. And then, there are such a series of unpretending, yet well arranged buildings, for the comfort, health and enjoyment of the inmates; so neatly kept throughout all their borders; and withal, so quiet and still, that one can hardly believe he is visiting an institution inhabited by hundreds of human beings, really insane. And he leaves it at last with the firm conviction that the superintendent, his aids and assistants, are marvellous persons indeed, who can keep so quiet, tidy and neat so many human beings, whose minds have so little control of their bodies, and the premises they occupy in such perfect order. Other institutions of the kind I have visited, of larger size, more costly, and of greater pretensions; but in all essential features, the New Hampshire Asylum for the Insane equals, if it does not exceed them all.

And the Lafayette monument will not only be known and honored in the State ; but throughout the whole country — from the great lakes to the greater gulf, and from the Atlantic to the Pacific oceans. **Concord** will become the Mecca of the nation, and pilgrims from afar will pay their devoirs at its shrine ; and, if latter-day prophets do not block the wheels of time, for many long ages yet to come.

Youths of America ! I linger, for I desire to proffer a few parting words. In pondering over this sketch, I doubt not, you have come to the conclusion, that Washington and Lafayette were needful to each other, and both *essential* to the success of the American revolution. Had either been wanting, it would have been a failure. Unlike in temperament, yet all the more useful aids to each other, and should be held in equal estimation, and alike honored by the American people.

In stern integrity, patriotism and noble daring, Gen. Lafayette had no superiors, and few equals, in the American Revolution. He had, indeed, in an eminent degree, the essential characteristics of a successful warrior—quick to perceive, sagacious to plan, and prompt to execute: While others shrunk from danger, and avoided all perilous positions, he bravely threw himself into the "deadly breach" and buffeted the storm of two revolutions, and became the bright, burnished link between two centuries, and the gallant HERO of two hemispheres. Let us, then, honor his name, imitate his virtues, and all join heart and hand to make this nation, what he prophesied it might be, one of the greatest nations of the earth. Let us then, with one voice and one mind, in trumpet tones proclaim, shout, sing —

> "Columbia, Columbia, to glory arise,
> The Queen of the world, and child of the skies."

I had concluded to stop here, and close my sketch of Gen. Lafayette; but, on reflection, I have thought that it might be deemed incomplete without some more particular notice of his many splendid receptions outside of New England. I have room only for a few of them; the whole would fill volumes. I begin with his

RECEPTION AT THE CITY OF HUDSON,

ON NORTH RIVER, STATE OF NEW YORK.

On landing at the wharf the crowd was so great that it was almost impossible to proceed in any direction, but by the great and active exertions of the marshal of the day, aided by military companies, Gen. Lafayette was conducted to an elegant barouche, drawn by four black horses, attended by four grooms in livery, and then proceeded up Warren street, at the head of which an arch had been erected, which, in size and elegance, exceeded anything that had been seen on the route. Half way up the street was another arch, more elegant than the first, and at the end was a third, superior to both! All along the street, more than a mile in length, a dense crowd cheered the General as he passed, and the ladies, in windows and on balconies, waved their handkerchiefs in the air, while Lafayette bowed, or attempted to bow, to the various individuals of that vast multitude.

The third arch claims a moment's notice. On its top, stood a colossal figure of the Goddess of Liberty, well proportioned and beautifully painted; holding in her hand the American standard, with a large flag that gracefully floated in the air. To all of the arches were suspended various and appropriate mottoes and inscriptions.

On arriving at the Court House, the troops opened to the right and left, and all that could, passed into the court-room. This room was most splendidly decorated throughout, displaying great labor, and uncommon taste and skill.

On each side of the entrance to the bar stood a beautiful corinthian pillar, with caps and cornices of the composite order, elegantly wrought and ornamented with leaves of gold. On the top of each of the pillars was placed a globe, and these were united by a chain of flowers of every hue, festooned with vases and laurels. At this enchanting portal, the Mayor gave the welcoming address, to which the General, with much emotion, replied. He was then introduced to the officers of the city, and ladies and gentlemen. But the most affecting scene was his introduction to sixty-eight veterans of the revolution. It so happened that some of them were officers, and many of them soldiers, who had served under Lafayette in the revolutionary army. Each had something to say; and, when they grasped his hand, were reluctant to release it. What each individual said cannot be recollected; but one said, You, General, gave me the first guinea I ever had in my life. Another presented the sword given him by the General in Rhode Island. But the feelings of the General and his comrades were too great for speech, and could only be relieved by sobs and tears.

As he passed down to the boat, he called at the hotel, where a sumptuous feast had been provided; but he could not stop to partake of it, as his dinner awaited him at Albany, and he was then some hours behind time. He, however, took a glass of wine and some refreshment, and passed on to the boat. When aboard, and the boat dashed out into the stream, cheers upon cheers were given by the vast multitude on shore, which were answered from the boat, while the cannons uttered their deep-toned voices from the hills. And thus, the boat was cheered from shore to shore on its route to Albany.

In some places the display was surprising—sometimes comical. On nearing the landing of a small village a solitary howitzer gave a national salute; and when the party were wondering what next, as no people were visible, a large cannon, concealed in the woods, answered it, while a multitude dashed down to the shore with loud shouts of welcome. And then a veteran soldier, whose enthusiasm could not be repressed, dashed down to the water's edge, fired his heavy loaded musket, swung his hat and shouted, "I give you, General, the best I've got." He was greeted from the boat with loud shouts of applause.

General Lafayette's trip extended to Troy; and he there visited Mrs. Willard's celebrated Ladies' Seminary. On arriving at the gate of the Institution he found an arbor of evergreens, extending to the building, a distance of 200 feet; and, on entering the house, he was presented to Mrs. Willard; and she then presented to him her pupils. On this occasion, two young ladies presented him the following poetic Address, composed by the principal; which was sung with great sweetness and pathos by Miss Eliza Smith, of Worcester, Mass. In the choruses, the pupils joined; and the whole was executed with great effect. The General was much moved; and at the close of the singing said: "I cannot express what I feel on this occasion; but will you, Madam, present me with three copies of these lines, to be given, as from you, to my three daughters?" The request, of course, was readily complied with.

LAFAYETTE'S WELCOME.

And art thou then, dear Hero, come?
  And do our eyes behold the man
Who nerved his arm and bared his breast
  For us, ere yet our life began?
For us, and for our native land,
  Thy youthful va'or dared the war;
And now, in winter of thine age,
  Have come, and left thy loved ones far.

Then, dear and deep thy welcome be,
Nor think thy daughters far from thee;
Columbia's daughters, lo! we bend,
And claim to call thee Father, Friend.

Nor yet, our country's rights alone
　Impelled thee on in Freedom's cause;
No, 'twas the love of human kind,
　Of human rights and equal laws.
It was benevolence sublime.
　Like that which moves the eternal mind;
And, benefactor of the world,
　He shed his blood for all mankind.

Then, deep and dear thy welcome be,
Nor think thy daughters far from thee!
Daughters of human kind, we bend,
And claim to call thee Father, Friend.

The General was then conducted back through the arbor, on the sides of which the pupils had arranged themselves in close order, to the number of two hundred, and threw laurels before him as he passed. The visit of Gen. Lafayette at Troy, short as it was, gave him great satisfaction, and he spoke of his visit at the seminary as one of the most interesting and delightful moments of his life.

RECEPTION AT THE LIVINGSTONS,
ON THE HUDSON.

When the steamer arrived at the landing, it was discovered that the groves were literally alive with people of all ages and sexes, shouting a welcome to the Nation's Guest. The rocks, glens, and even the trees to their topmost branches, were full of joyous people, who joined in the general shouts of joy. The General was escorted to the ancient mansion house of the Livingstons, then occupied by Robert L. Livingston; and after a short time of introductions, a splendid picnic was served to the multitude.

He was then conducted to the more modern, but not less elegant, mansion of Edward P. Livingston. Among the most attractive displays here, was a sumptuous supper, served up in a style seldom if ever equalled in this country. The place selected for this fete, was an extensive green-house, or orangery, and the effect was very imposing. The tables had been made for the occasion, and placed beneath a grove of lemon and orange trees, full of fruit, and brilliantly lighted by hundreds of lamps; while on the outside, the whole atmosphere was, at times, splendidly lighted up by fireworks. This enchanting scene was ended by a dance, which lasted far into night; but the General early retired for his much needed rest.

RECEPTION AT NEWARK, N. J.

The General's reception at Newark was very unique and imposing. As the procession moved to the green, surrounded by troops, it was met by 24 male singers ranged in two lines, who sung with great pathos the following lines :—

Hail to the Gallant Chief, whose fame
Is pure as Heaven's etherial flame!
Millions of grateful people cheer
And welcome our brave soldier here.
O! strew the blooms of vale and grove,
Bright as our joys, warm as our love;
The present and the past are met
To welcome noble Lafayette.

The General, followed by the procession, passed through the centre of the green until he came near a magnificent bower, where he was received by 24 female singers, ranged in the same order as the men singers, who tuned their voices to the following strain :—

We weave the wreath, we pour the wine,
Where smiles like sparkling sunbeams shine;
And hail the thousands fondly met
To greet thee, matchless Lafayette!
Unseen, around the flowery way
Shades of the dead in glory play;
While hearts beat high and eyes are wet;
The winds of heaven hail Lafayette!

The General then passed on between the lines of these ladies, who strewed his pathway with flowers; and entered a splendid rural temple, erected for his reception. The base of the temple was 40 feet in diameter, in front of which was a beautiful portico, composed of 13 arches, representing the 13 original States, over which was a dome, representing the Western hemisphere. The pillars which sustained the dome were 15 feet in height, and wreathed with evergreens and flowers. On both sides, and directly back, were colonnades of twelve arches, forming arbors for the ladies. The tower was lofty, and supported by four triumphal arches; on the summit stood a large golden eagle, with a crown of laurel in his beak, and an olive branch on the liberty cap which he held in his talons. In front of the portico, was the name of La-fayette in large letters, made with white blossoms. In the centre was a platform on which were two large chairs; and over the one occupied by the General, was a canopy in the form of a cone, wreathed with brilliant flowers of various hues. On the arches forming the portico, were the following inscriptions: *on the West*, "Now I am going to serve you;" *on the South*, "For him whom the nation delights to honor;" *on the North*, "We ne'er shall look on his like again;" *on the East*, "His laurels shall never fade."

The workmanship of this temple was as neat as the design was classical. Everything was interwoven with such skill and compactness as to form cornices, capitals, and fretwork, with as much exactness as could be made in sculptured marble. It was, indeed, a fairy palace as seen at a distance, and resembled the beautiful palace in the garden of Versailles in France, which it was designed to imitate.

The foregoing account is but an item in the display at Newark; but by this, judge the rest.

RECEPTION AT PHILADELPHIA, PA.

Early in the morning, the General left Frankford for Philadelphia, distant five miles. The population of the city poured forth to meet him, in carriages, on horseback and on foot, and filled every avenue for the whole distance; while the windows, balconies and platforms were filled with ladies—all joyous and shouting welcomes. But human voices could not give full utterance to the feelings of overflowing hearts. In a field of 50 acres, near the city, a division of militia, 5500 strong, composed of cavalry, artillery and infantry, were drawn up in a hollow square to meet him; and his approach was announced by 100 rounds of artillery. The General proceeded in his carriage to the centre; arose, and waved his hat and bowed to the troops all around him in succession, while salutes and shouts of welcome, loud and long, greeted him on all sides. He made the review on foot, but received the saluting honors in his carriage.

The line of march was then taken for the city, and the procession was more than three miles long. A full description of this procession, and the numerous decorations and arches on the route, cannot be given in detail. A mere outline must suffice.

1. A cavalcade of 100 citizens.
2. One hundred mounted field and staff officers.
3. Five hundred cavalry troops.
4. A mounted band of music.
5. A company of 150 cavalry.
6. A brigade of 2000 militia.
7. Committee of arrangements on horseback.
8. General Lafayette and Judge Petters, in a splendid barouche.
9. Four other barouches, with Govs. Shultze and Williamson and suites, the General's family, and other distinguished individuals.

10.   Three cars of large size, splendidly decorated, made for the occasion, containing 120 revolutionary heroes. Each carriage had the name of Washington in front, and Lafayette in the rear; and on one side, "Defenders of the country," and on the other, "The survivors of 1776."

11.   Four hundred young men on foot.

12.   Various trades, led by a car of printers at work, both at the case and press, and printing and distributing patriotic odes.

13.   Typographical Society, with banner, Lafayette.

14.   Two hundred shoemakers, with banners, badges and emblems.

15.   Three hundred weavers, with decorations.

16.   One hundred and fifty rope-makers, with emblems.

17.   One hundred and fifty lads dressed in uniform.

18.   One hundred ship-builders, with banners.

19.   Seven hundred mechanics of various occupations.

20.   One hundred and fifty coopers, fitting staves and driving hoops.

21.   One hundred and fifty butchers, mounted, and in white frocks.

22.   Two hundred and sixty truckmen, mounted, with white aprons trimmed with blue.

23.   One hundred and fifty rifle men, in frocks.

24.   A full company of artillery, with two field-pieces.

25.   A brigade of 1800 infantry.

26.   A company of New Jersey cavalry.

27.   The Red Men of the State.

28.   The Lafayette Society.

29.   "The True Republican Association."

30.   "The German American Association."

31.   A body of 300 sturdy farmers concluded the procession.

The appearance of this grand procession was august and imposing. As it passed, "LAFAYETTE, LAFAY-

15

ETTE!" sprang from the voices of a multitude that rolled on, and on, and on, like the waves of the ocean, in numbers estimated at a quarter of a million. Lafayette beat in every heart; Lafayette hung on every tongue; Lafayette glowed on every cheek; Lafayette glistened in every eye, and swelled on every gale. The country and the whole city appeared arrayed in all their glory, beauty and strength; at once, to witness and adore the majesty of the spectacle and to honor the Nation's Guest.

The procession, after passing through the principal streets of Philadelphia, halted in front of the old State House, in which was signed the Declaration of Independence in 1776. Here, the General alighted, passed under a most magnificent triumphal arch into the hall, which had been decorated in a most splendid manner for this occasion. Among the decorations was a statue of Washington, and portraits of William Penn, Dr. Franklin, Robert Morris, Francis Hopkinson, Generals Greene, Wayne, Montgomery, Hamilton, Gates, Rochambeau; and also, of Charles Carroll of Carrollton, Jefferson, Hancock, Adams, Madison, Munroe, and Thompson. Here were assembled the city authorities, the society of Cincinnati, the judges of the courts, &c., &c. The mayor of the city then gave him a most eloquent address, to which the General gave a feeling reply, in a faltering voice, for he was manifestly overcome by his emotions.

At night, the whole city was brilliantly illuminated; in which the United States Bank building presented a most enchanted appearance. The lights were so placed as not to be seen, and the doors being thrown open, it appeared like a palace of transparent marble.

Among the numerous arches was one of gigantic size and splendid appearance, after the plan of one of the famous arches of Rome. It was constructed of wood, covered with canvas, and painted in perfect imitation of stone.

Its front was forty-five feet, embracing a basement story of doric order, from which an arch sprung to the height of twenty-four feet. The spandrels on each front were decorated with the figure of Fame painted in elegant style, with arms extended and holding a civic crown over the key stone. The wings were of the Ionic order, and decorated with statues of Liberty, Victory, Independence and Plenty, with suitable mottoes; the whole surmounted with an entablature of thirty feet. In the centre, under the arms of the city, and on each side, were placed the statues of Wisdom and Justice, with appropriate emblems. The superficial surface of painted canvas exceeded 3000 feet.

The next day, a grand levee was held in the State House, where thousands took him by the hand; and he received no less than fourteen addresses: one each from the Old Soldiers, Philosophical and Bible Societies, the University, Chamber of Commerce, the Bar, the Young Men, the French Citizens, the Washington Grays, the Lafayette Association, the Revolutionary Officers, and the Young Ladies of the several schools.

A grand civic ball was given in the new theatre, exceeding anything of the kind ever witnessed in the city before. Seventeen hundred ladies and gentlemen were present, exhibiting an unrivalled galaxy of elegance and splendor. But the details of this brilliant assembly cannot be given in words, and must be left to the imagination. Of the company present were Mrs. Robert Morris, the two Misses Bollman, daughters of Dr. Erick Bollman, Gov. Schultze, Gov. Williamson, John Quincy Adams, Gen. Barnard, and two hundred citizens from the various States of the Union, together with thousands of joyful spectators.

The next day a most beautiful spectacle was exhibited in the State House yard, where 2000 school children were assembled, all dressed in uniform, to greet and receive an address from Gen. Lafayette.

In fine, we must cut short this interesting display, and leave it half untold. Suffice it to say, the General spent six days at Philadelphia in one continual round of visits and receptions, unequalled, perhaps, in the annals of time, and departed, at last, amid the roar of cannon and shouts of the multitude, for Washington city.

RECEPTION AT BALTIMORE, MD.

After leaving Philadelphia, the General passed through the principal towns of Delaware, where he was enthusiastically received, and arrived at Frenchtown in the evening, and went on board the steamer United States, which had come down from Baltimore to receive him. On board the boat, he was highly entertained by his friends, and staid all night. Here, he had an unexpected meeting with his old friend, Capt. Du Boismarten, who procured for him, and commanded the vessel that first landed him in this country in 1777. The Captain was a venerable Frenchman of 83 winters, many of which had been cheerless and bleak, for he was sadly poor. He was greatly overcome in meeting Gen. Lafayette, and left him, at last, with a lighter heart and heavier purse.

The next morning, the boat proceeded to Baltimore, and on entering the Patapsco river was met by five steamers, all beautifully dressed for the occasion, full of joyous ladies and gentlemen, which sailed round the steamer United States, and cheered the General as they passed. These five steamers then rounded to, and followed in the wake of the United States to Fort McHenry, where Gen. Lafayette was to make his headquarters while in Baltimore.

The General was received on the platform of the Fort

by Col. Hindman, of the U. S. Army, where the 36th and 38th Regiments had their stations. On entering the gate, the troops opened to the right and left, which brought to view the identical tent of Gen. Washington, used by him in the revolutionary war. Here Gov. Stevens greeted him with an animated address. He was then conducted into the tent, where he found members of the Cincinnati, and patriarchs of the revolution. The meeting was most affecting; the General embraced them all, and all were convulsed with tears of gratulation and joy.

When the first emotions had subsided, Lafayette cast his eyes round the tent, and discovering a part of the well known camp equipage of Washington, in a subdued voice said, "I remember, I remember! Language cannot express my feelings in meeting my brothers in arms in the tent of Washington." There was silence and tears in the tent for a time.

The company then proceeded to an adjoining marquee, where breakfast had been prepared for the occasion. At the close of this repast, the General was conducted to a most splendid two seated barouche, made expressly for the occasion, and exceeding in beauty anything of the kind in America; which was presented to the General when he left by the makers, and he took it with him on his Southern tour. The venerable Charles Carroll of Carrollton, Gen. Smith, and Col. Howard, took seats in the carriage with Gen. Lafayette; and when it left the outer gate of the fort was met by a thousand cavalry, which formed his escort through the city. In passing Federal Hill, a salute of twenty-four guns was fired to denote the number of States in the Union. After passing under splendid arches, the General beheld, at the head of Market street, ten thousand men, in companies, completely armed and in full uniform. Here, all his companions left the carriage, and the General, alone in the barouche, passed along the whole line, then took a fair position, and the troops passed in review before him. The appearance of Market street was most animated and splendid—every house-top, window, balcony, door and sidewalk being filled with joyous spectators.

The city of Baltimore was filled by a vast multitude of people as never before nor since; yet the utmost order prevailed, and the General was greeted throughout all the streets with all the tokens of welcome that human feelings or ingenuity could bestow.

At the Exchange, he was received and addressed by the Mayor, and introduced to the Councils, and others. He then proceeded to a pavilion on Light street, at the entrance into Market street, where he received the final passing salutes of the military companies. Language would fail to describe this splendid pageantry, which lasted nearly two hours.

At 5 o'clock a sumptuous feast had been provided, at which the Mayor presided. Among the guests were Wm. Patterson, Gov. John B. Morris, John Quincy Adams, then Secretary of State; Gen. Macomb, of the U. S. Army; Col. Howard, Gen. Samuel Smith, Geo. Washington Custis of Arlington; Generals Stricker, Stuart, Reed, Benson, Harper, Stansbury and McDonald; the Colonels commanding regiments in the State and city, together with a large number of guests from the various States in the Union.

In the procession, was proudly borne the standard of the brave Count Pulaski, who fell at the assault on Savannah, fastened to one of the spears of his legion, to which his sword was attached by his cross-belt, now in the possession of Col. Bentalo, as an affectionate memorial of his departed friend.

In the evening, the city illumination was most splendid; especially, the Exchange, Dispensary, Banks, Theatre and

Museum, and the arches were in a full blaze of light; while pyramids of fire at the bridge, and a revolving star, three feet in diameter, had an imposing effect, hard to describe. The whole scene was interspersed with transparencies, mottoes and devices, all appropriate to the occasion.

The ball-room in the evening was most splendidly decorated and illuminated. After the ceremony of introducing the General to the ladies and gentlemen was over, at the signal of a bugle blast, the dancing instantly began. In time, supper was announced, and the managers escorted the General into a hall no less splendid than the ball-room itself. The cheerful conviviality, appropriate and cordial hilarity, may be considered as the finishing touch to the magnificent fete at Baltimore.

The addresses to and from General Lafayette were so numerous, that I have given them merely a passing notice; but the official addresses at the seat of government in Washington city, I give entire.

ADDRESS OF SPEAKER CLAY,
IN THE HOUSE OF REPRESENTATIVES, DEC. 10, 1824.

GENERAL: The House of Representatives of the United States, impelled alike by their own feelings and by those of the whole American people, could not have assigned me a more gratifying duty than of being its organ to present to you cordial congratulations upon the occasion of your recent arrival in the United States, in compliance with the wishes of Congress; and to assure you of the high satisfaction which your presence affords on this early theatre of your glory and renown. Although but few of the members who compose this body shared with you, in the war of the revolution, all have a knowledge from impartial history, or from faithful tradition, of the perils,

the sufferings and sacrifices, which you have voluntarily
encountered, and the signal services in America and in
Europe which you performed for an infant, a distant and
an alien people, and all feel and own the very great extent
of the obligations under which you have placed this country. But the relations in which you have ever stood to
the United States, interesting and important as they have
been, do not constitute the only motive of the respect and
admiration which the House entertains for you. Your
consistency of character, your uniform devotion to regulated liberty, in all the vicissitudes of a long and arduous
life, also commands its highest admiration. During all
the recent convulsions of Europe, amidst, as after the
dispersion of, every political storm, the people of the
United States have ever beheld you true to your old principles, firm and erect, cheering and animating with your
well known voice the votaries of liberty, its faithful and
fearless champion, ready to shed the last drop of that
blood which you so freely and nobly spilled in the same
holy cause.

The vain wish has sometimes been indulged, that Providence would allow the Patriot, after death, to return to
his country, and to contemplate the infermediate changes
which had taken place—to view the forests felled, the
cities built, the mountains leveled, the canals cut, the
highways constructed, the progress of the arts, the ad-
vancement of learning, and the increase of population.
General, your present visit to the United States is the
consoling object of that wish. You are in the midst of
posterity. Everywhere you must have been struck with
the great changes, physical and moral, which have occurred
since you left us. Even this very city, bearing a venerated name alike endeared to you and to us, has since
emerged from the forest which then covered its site. In
one respect, you behold us unaltered, and that is in this

sentiment of continued devotion to liberty, and of ardent
affection and profound gratitude to your departed friend,
the Father of this Country, and to your illustrious associates in the field and in the cabinet, for the multiplied
blessings which surround us, and for the very privilege
of addressing you, which I now exercise. This sentiment,
now fondly cherished by more than ten millions of people,
will be transmitted, with unabated vigor, down the tide
of time, through the countless millions who are destined
to inhabit this continent, to the latest posterity.

GENERAL LAFAYETTE'S REPLY.

MR. SPEAKER, AND GENTLEMEN OF THE HOUSE OF
REPRESENTATIVES: While the people of the United
States, and their honorable Representatives in Congress,
have deigned to make choice of me, one of the American
veterans, to signify in his person their esteem for our
joint services, and their attachment to the principles for
which we have had the honor to fight and bleed, I am
proud and happy to share these extraordinary favors with
my dear revolutionary companions; and yet, it would be
on my part uncandid and ungrateful not to acknowledge
my personal share in these testimonials of kindness, as
they excite in my breast emotions which no adequate words
can express.

My obligations to the United States, sir, far exceed
any merit I might claim. They date from the time I had
the happiness to be adopted as a young soldier, a favored
son of America. They have been continued to me during
almost half a century of constant affection and confidence;
and now, sir, thanks to your most gratifying invitation, I
find myself greeted by a series of welcomes, one hour of
which would more than compensate for all the public exertions and sufferings of a whole life.

The approbation of the American people, and their

16

Representatives, for my conduct during the vicissitudes of the European revolution, is the highest reward I could receive. Well may I stand firm and erect, when in their names, and by you, Mr. Speaker, I am declared to have, in every instance, been faithful to those American principles of liberty, equality, and true social order—the devotion to which, as it has been from my earliest youth, so shall it continue to be to my latest breath.

You have been pleased, Mr. Speaker, to allude to the peculiar felicity of my situation, when, after so long an absence, I am called to witness the immense improvements, the admirable communications, the prodigious creations, of which I find an example in this city, whose name itself is a venerated palladium; in a word, all the grandeur and prosperity of these happy States, which reflect on every part of the world a superior political civilization.

What better pledge can be given of a continued national love of liberty, where these blessings are evidently the result of a virtuous resistance to oppression, and the institutions founded on the rights of man, and the republican principles of self-government. No, Mr. Speaker, posterity has not begun for me, since in the sons of my companions and friends, I find the same public feelings, and permit me to add, the same feelings in my behalf, which I have had the happiness to experience in their fathers.

Sir, forty years ago, to a Congress of thirteen States, I was allowed to express the fond wishes of an American heart. On this day I have the honor, and enjoy the delight of congratulating the Representatives of the Union, so vastly enlarged, on the realization of those wishes, even beyond every human expectation, and upon the almost infinite prospects we can with certainty anticipate.

Permit me, Mr. Speaker, and Gentlemen of the House of Representatives, to join to the expression of those sentiments, a tribute of my profound gratitude, devotion and respect.

FAREWELL ADDRESS OF PRESIDENT JOHN QUINCY ADAMS.

SEPTEMBER 6, 1825.

GENERAL LAFAYETTE : It has been the good fortune of many of my distinguished fellow-citizens, during the course of the year now elapsed, upon your arrival at their respective places of abode, to greet you with the welcome of the nation. The less pleasing task now devolves upon me, of bidding you, in the name of the nation, Adieu.

It were no longer seasonable, and would be superfluous, to recapitulate the remarkable incidents of your early life— incidents which associated your name, fortunes, and repu- tation, in imperishable connection with the independence and history of the North American Union.

The part which you performed at that important junc- ture was marked with characters so peculiar, that, realiz- ing the fairest fable of antiquity, its parallel could scarcely be found in the *authentic* records of human history.

You deliberately and perseveringly preferred toil, dan- ger, the endurance of every hardship, and the privation of every comfort, in defence of a holy cause, to inglorious ease, and the allurements of rank, affluence, and unre- strained youth, at the most splendid and fascinating Court of Europe.

That this choice was not less wise than magnanimous, the sanction of half a century, and the gratulations of unnumbered voices, all unable to express the gratitude of the heart with which your visit to this hemisphere has been welcomed, afford ample demonstration.

When the contest of freedom, to which you had repaired as a voluntary champion, had closed, by the complete tri- umph of her cause in this country of your adoption, you returned to fulfil the duties of the philanthropist and patriot in the land of your nativity. There, in a consis- tent and undeviating career of forty years, you have maintained, through every vicissitude of alternate success and disappointment, the same glorious cause to which the first years of your active life had been devoted, the improvement of the moral and political condition of man.

Throughout that long succession of time, the people of the United States, for whom, and with whom, you had fought the battles of liberty, have been living in the full possession of its fruits; one of the happiest among the family of nations. Spreading in population; enlarging in territory; acting and suffering according to the condition of their nature; and laying the foundations of the greatest, and, we humbly hope, the most beneficent power that ever regulated the concerns of man upon earth.

In that lapse of forty years, the generation of men with whom you co-operated in the conflict of arms, has nearly passed away. Of the general officers of the American army in that war, you alone survive. Of the sages who guided our councils; of the warriors who met the foe in the field or upon the wave, with the exception of a few, to whom unusual length of days has been allotted by Heaven, all now sleep with their fathers. A succeeding, and even a third generation, have arisen to take their places; and their children's children, while rising up to call them blessed, have been taught by them, as well as admonished by their own constant enjoyment of freedom, to include in every benison upon their fathers, the name of him who came from afar, with them and in their cause, to conquer or to fall.

The universal prevalence of these sentiments was signally manifested by a resolution of Congress, representing the whole people, and all the States of this Union, requesting the President of the United States to communicate to you the assurances of grateful and affectionate attachment of this government and people, and desiring that a national ship might be employed, at your convenience, for your passage to the borders of our country.

The invitation was transmitted to you by my venerable predecessor; himself bound to you by the strongest ties of personal friendship; himself one of those whom the highest honors of his country had rewarded for blood early shed in her cause, and for a long life of devotion to her welfare. By him the services of a national ship were placed at your disposal. Your delicacy preferred a more private conveyance, and a full year has elapsed since you landed upon our shores. It were scarcely an exaggeration to say, that it has been, to the people of the Union, a year of uninterrupted festivity and enjoyment, inspired by your presence. You have traversed the twenty-four States of this Confederacy. You have been received with rapture by the survivors of your earliest companions in arms. You have been hailed as a long absent parent by their children, the men and women of the present age. And a rising generation, the hope of future time, in numbers surpassing the whole population of that day when you fought at the head and by the side of their forefathers, have vied with the scanty remnants of that hour of trial, in acclamations of joy beholding the face of him whom they feel to be the common benefactor of all. You have heard the mingled voices of the past, the present, and the future age, joining in one universal chorus of delight at your approach; and the shouts of unbidden thousands, which greeted your landing on the soil of freedom, have followed every step of your way, and still resound, like the rushing of many waters, from every corner of our land.

You are now about to return to the country of your birth, of your ancestors, of your posterity. The executive government of the Union, stimulated by the same feeling which had prompted the Congress to the designation of a national ship for your accommodation in coming hither, has destined the first service of a frigate, recently launched at this metropolis, to the less welcome, but equally distinguished trust, of conveying you home. The name of the ship has added one more memorial to distant regions and to future ages, of a stream already memorable, at once in the story of your sufferings and of our independence.

The ship is now prepared for your reception, and equipped for sea. From the moment of her departure, the prayers of millions will ascend to Heaven that her passage may be prosperous, and your return to the bosom of your family as propitious to your happiness, as your visit to this scene of your youthful glory has been to that of the American people.

Go, then, our beloved friend—return to the land of brilliant genius, of generous sentiment, of heroic valor; to that beautiful France, the nursing mother of the twelfth Louis and the fourth Henry; to the native soil of Bayard and Coligni, of Turenne and Catinat, of Fenelon and D'Aguesseau. In that illustrious catalogue of names which she claims as of her children, and with honest pride holds up to the admiration of other nations, the name of Lafayette has already for centuries been enrolled. And it shall henceforth burnish into brighter fame; for if, in after days, a Frenchman shall be called to indicate the character of his nation by that of one individual, during the age in which we live, the blood of lofty patriotism shall mantle in his cheek, the fire of conscious virtue shall sparkle in his eye, and he shall pronounce the name of Lafayette. Yet we too, and our children, in life and after death, shall claim you for our own. You are ours by that more than patriotic self-devotion with which you flew to the aid of our fathers at the crisis of their fate. Ours by that long series of years in which you have cherished us in your regard. Ours by the unshaken sentiment of gratitude for your services

which is a precious portion of our inheritance. Ours by
that tie of love, stronger than death, which has linked
your name, for the endless ages of time, with the name
of WASHINGTON.

At the painful moment of parting from you, we take
comfort in the thought, that wherever you may be, to the
last pulsation of your heart, our country will be ever
present to your affections; and a cheering consolation
assures us, that we are not called to sorrow most of all,
that we shall see your face no more. We shall indulge
the pleasing anticipation of beholding our friend again.
In the meantime, speaking in the name of the whole
people of the United States, and at a loss only for language to give utterance to that feeling of attachment with
which the heart of the nation beats, as the heart of one
man—I bid you a reluctant and affectionate farewell.

GENERAL LAFAYETTE'S REPLY.

Amidst all my obligations to the General Government,
and particularly to you, Sir, its respected Chief Magistrate, I have most thankfully to acknowledge the opportunity given me, at this solemn and painful moment, to
present to the people of the United States, with a parting
tribute of profound, inexpressible gratitude.

To have been, in the important and critical days of those
States, adopted by them as a favorite son; to have par-
ticipated with them in the toils and perils of our unspot-
ted struggle for independence, freedom and equal rights;
and, in the foundation of the American era, of a new social order, which has already pervaded this, and must, for
the dignity and happiness of mankind, successively per-
vade every part of the other hemisphere; to have received
at every stage of the revolution, and during forty years
after that period, from the people of the United States,
and their Representatives, at home and abroad, continued

marks of their confidence and kindness, has been the pride, the encouragement, the support of a long and eventful life.

But how can I find words to acknowledge that series of welcomes, those unbounded and universal displays of public affection, which have marked each step, each hour of the twelve months' progress through the twenty-four States; and which, while they overwhelm my heart with grateful delight, have most satisfactorily evinced the concurrence of the people in the kind testimonies, in the immense favors bestowed upon me by the several branches of their Representatives, in every part, and at the central seat of the Confederacy.

Yet, gratifications still higher await me, in the wonders of creation and improvement that have met my enchanted eye; in the unparalled and self-felt happiness of the people, in their rapid prosperity and insured security, public and private; in the practice of good order, the appendage of true freedom and a national good sense, the final arbiter of all difficulties. I have had proudly to recognize a result of the republican principles for which we have fought, and a glorious demonstration to the most timid and prejudicial mind, of the superiority over degrading aristocracy or despotism, of popular institutions, founded on the plain rights of man, and where the local rights of every section are preserved under a constitutional bond of union. The cherishing of that union between the States, as it has been the farewell entreaty of our great paternal Washington, and will ever have the dying prayer of every patriotic American; so it has become the sacred pledge of the emancipation of the world; an object in which, I am happy to observe that the American people, while they give the animating example of successful free institutions in return for an evil entailed upon them by Europe; and of which a liberal and enlightened sense is everywhere more and more generally felt, show themselves every day more anxiously interested.

And now, Sir, how can I do justice to my deep feelings, for the assurances, most peculiarly valued, of your esteem and friendship; for your kind references to old times, to my beloved associates, to the vicissitudes of my life, for your affectionate picture of the blessings poured by the several generations of the American people on the remaining days of a delighted veteran, for your affectionate remarks on this sad hour of separation, on the country of my birth, full I can say of American sympathies; on the hope, so necessary for me, of seeing again the country that had deigned, near half a century ago, to call me hers! I shall content myself, refraining from superfluous repetitions, at once before you, Sir, and this respected circle, to proclaim my cordial confirmation of every one of the sentiments which I have had daily opportunities publicly to utter, from the time when your remarkable predecessor, my old friend and brother in arms, transmitted to me the honorable invitation of Congress, to this day, when you, my dear Sir, whose friendly connections with me, date from your earliest youth, are going to consign me to the protection across the Atlantic, of the heroic national flag, on board the splendid ship "Brandywine," the name of which has been not the least flattering and kind, among the numberless favors conferred upon me.

God bless you, Sir, and all who surround us. God bless the American people, each of their States, and the Federal Government. Accept this patriotic farewell of an overflowing heart—such will be its last throb when it ceases to beat.

———

At the close of the President's address, the General embraced him in his arms, saluting him in the French manner on each cheek. And on pronouncing the last sentence of his answer, he advanced, and while the tears poured over his venerable cheeks, again took the President in his arms. He retired a few paces, but, overcome by his feelings, again returned, uttering in a broken voice, and with great emotion, "*God bless you; farewell; God bless you!*" The scene was at once solemn and moving; as the sighs and stealing tears of many—nay, of all—who witnessed it bore testimony. The greetings were continued, when self-possession had been recovered, till each individual had shared in the pledge of kindness. In bidding adieu to one of the sons of Mr. Adams, whom the General long held by the hand, his eyes beamed with paternal affection. With Mr. Clay, whose countenance gave token that he had not escaped the "soft infection," the General held much converse; and while the refreshments of the hospitable mansion were in circulation, the company gathered around the Guest, to take another and yet another farewell look, and to seize once more "that beloved hand which was opened so freely for our aid when aid was so precious, and which grasped with firm and undeviating hold, the steel which so essentially helped to achieve our deliverance."

The procession being formed, a salute of 24 guns announced the order for its movement. On the appearance of the President, with the guest, in the Court in front of the house, a general salute was given to the President by the troops.

The General was then attended to his barouche by Messrs. Clay, Southard and Rush, who rode with him. The procession then moved in the prescribed order; the brigades of volunteers passing before the President in review.

When arrived near where the "Mount Vernon" steamboat was gallantly riding on the Potomac to receive him, the guest took a station, in his barouche, when the whole

military escort, commanded by Gen. Smith, passed him
in review, paying him the customary honors. After this,
Mrs. Custis, Mrs. Lewis, (of the Washington family,)
and other friends, took their leave individually. He then
descended, and was escorted to the steamer,* which at
half past three o'clock moved from the wharf, under a
farewell salute of 24 guns, the huzzas of many thousands
crowning the eminences, and the broken shouts of scattered
multitudes assembled on the shores.

As the boat passed the Point, the Navy Yard and the
Fort, salutes were fired in succession; and the shouts of
adieu continued till the boat was entirely lost to the view.
Thus terminated a day which memory and history will
cherish, and which will be reverted to with feelings of
pride and rapture by our descendants, when those who
were the actors in it shall have passed from the theatre of
human existence.

It is now a hundred years since Gen. Lafayette first set
his foot on American soil, and more than half a century
since his last visit. But few now living have ever seen
him; and less memorials of him than of Washington now
remain. And as Lafayette was a foreigner, and but a few
years in this country, he never was so well known as
Washington. Nor has he been so fortunate as to have a
Marshall, Sparks or Washington Irving to write his life
and times. Small volumes and brief sketches have been
published, but very incomplete, and sometimes erroneous.

----

* In explanation of the guest's going on board a steamer at the
Navy Yard, it should be stated that the Brandywine, in which he
was to embark and return to France, was a sailing vessel, depend-
ing on the wind, and of such a large size that it could not be readily
handled in the upper waters of the Potomac; and therefore it was
anchored some 20 miles down the stream, where the river was much
larger and the water deeper.

Nor has he ever to the public appeared or been esteemed at his real worth. Many have supposed that as he was an impulsive Frenchman, he was fickle-minded and superficial. But he was very far from all this; for he was a man of a strong mind, a deep thinker and a ripe scholar. Impulsive he was, and did nothing by halves; but what his hand found to do that ought to be done, he did with all his might. That less should be known of him than of Washington, is no marvel. And far be it from me to eulogize the one at the expense of the other.

In early life I was taught to venerate the name of the Father of his Country, who was pronounced to be first in war, first in peace, and first in the hearts of his countrymen. It is said that republics are ungrateful. Whatever truth there may have been in ancient republics, ours does not come under that condemnation.

In early manhood, I lived three years in the State of Virginia. In that time, I travelled much over the State; and, in addition to its curiosities and matchless scenery, I visited the place of Washington's birth, on what is called the "Northern Neck," in the County of Westmoreland, between the Potomac and Rappahannock rivers. The house in which he was born was in ruins; as was also the house where he and his widowed mother had lived, opposite to the city of Fredericksburg. He was said to have been an athletic youth, and beat all his associates in sports that required great muscular strength, such as leaping and tossing the bar. He was said to have been the only youth that could cast a stone across the Rappahannock river at Fredericksburg. I tried my hand at it, but could throw a stone only about two-thirds of that distance. His mother spent her last days in that city, and was there buried.

I also beheld, with awe and veneration, Mount Vernon, the home of Washington, and the tomb where his mortal remains repose. These scenes impressed me profoundly at the time, as the remembrance of them does now.

And, moreover, the patriotic ladies of the land, in 1858, formed a society called the "Ladies' Mount Vernon Association," appointed agents throughout the whole country, raised money by subscription and donation, and purchased Mount Vernon with two hundred acres of land, at the large price of two hundred thousand dollars. Two hundred thousand dollars is a large sum to be raised by voluntary contribution, but the patriotic ladies were equal to the task. They induced the great orator, Edward Everett, to write and deliver throughout the land, one of the most touching and eloquent lectures on Washington that was ever written. And this lecture was delivered in the principal towns and cities *sixty-five* times! One might well suppose that a lecture, continually repeated by the author, would in time pall upon the senses, and become tame and insipid, and listlessly delivered. But the tradition is, that he stood up to the work like a martyr, and delivered it the last time with the same energy and pathos as at the first. And all this was done without any compensation to himself, and the large sums obtained as admission fees, were added to the purchasing funds.

And this Association of ladies, having completed the purchase of Mount Vernon; by their agent, now occupy the premises, put the same in complete repair, as in the days of Washington, and dedicated it to the nation as a place of public resort and pilgrimage forever.

And now what more can be said or done in regard to Washington? In his case, surely, the republic has not been ungrateful.

As to General Lafayette, what more can be done to show a nation's gratitude? Lagrange, his beautiful home in France, is not purchasable, as his posterity still occupy; and if it could be, it is in a foreign country, and could not be made a place of resort for the American people. But these pages will show abundant manifestations of gratitude to Gen. Lafayette, and nothing now seems needful to be done but to erect monuments to his memory, the same as to Washington himself. There is not so much said or done in regard to Lafayette as in former times, for the present generation do not know him as well, and I feel that he ought to be known and esteemed as in times past. To this end have I written, and I hope not in vain.

And now, most respectfully, I dedicate this brief sketch of the life of Gen. Lafayette to the youth of America, in the hope and fervent wish that his noble life will influence theirs, even more than it has that of the author. If that wish should be gratified, we shall have no more selfish, narrow-minded and dishonest politicians ; but honest men and true patriots will bear rule, and the country will become, what Gen. Lafayette prayed it might, the greatest and most glorious nation on earth.

MAJOR ANDRE.

[The following Sketch of the unfortunate Maj. Andre was written in 1821, and published in the newspapers of the time. It gives so much more information of him than the brief notice in my " Recollections," that I insert the article entire.]

As the gallant, amiable but unfortunate Major Andre has again been brought into notice by the removal of his remains from Tappan, a notice of the causes which led him to join the army in America and his ignominious exit on a gibbet, may not at this time be unacceptable. His family resided at Claptan near London for the most part

of the time; and consisted of his mother, three sisters—
Maria, Anna and Louisa—and his brother William. They
were very respectable, moved in the first circles and had
many friends; for there seems to have been something
very fascinating and cordial in their manners, together
with an engaging personal appearance that riveted the
affections of all their acquaintances. The family were
well acquainted at Litchfield, a pleasant village, 120 miles
from their residence, and took much delight in their visits
there; especially John Andre, the hero of our story. He
seems to have been formed by nature to love and be
beloved. His personal appearance was noble and fascinating, and his acquirements were such as to give an additional attraction to the advantages of nature. He had
invoked the muses with considerable success, and was a
musician and painter. He was a belles lettres scholar and
well versed in history and politics; and in short, his
acquirements were such as to enable him to shine in any
circle, and become, as in fact he did, the idol of his family
and friends. At the age of eighteen, he became more
particularly attached to a young lady of Litchfield, by the
name of Honora Snyed. His attachment appears to have
been something more than the evanescent kind, which
vanishes with its object; for it neither abated nor dimin-
ished by time or distance, but continued to the last
moment of his life. It appears, he was not indifferent to
his fair Honora; she received his addresses, and avowed
a reciprocal attachment. Honora's health at this time was
very delicate; so much so, that she was forbidden to correspond with any one; the intercourse between them was
continued, however, through the medium of her sister
Anna, in whose letters Honora would add a postscript.

As the family did not possess an independent fortune,
Maj. Andre established himself in the mercantile business
in Warnford Court, London. The drudgery of a count-

ing-room illy agreed with his ardent imagination, and nothing but the soothing idea, that he was acquiring property to share with his Honora, rendered his situation tolerable. He is sometimes very pleasant and sportive in his letters to Anna Snyed; and in a measure, seems to have overcome his dislike to the occupation of a merchant. He says :—

"I no longer see it in so disadvantageous a light. Instead of figuring a merchant as a middle-aged man, with a bob wig, a rough beard, in snuff-colored clothes, grasping a guinea in his red hand; I conceive a comely young man, with a tolerable pig-tail, wielding a pen with all the noble fierceness of the Duke of Marlborough brandishing a truncheon on a sign-post, surrounded with types and emblems, and canopied with cornucopias that disembogue their stores upon his head; Mercurys reclined upon bales of goods; Genii playing with pens, ink and paper; while in perspective his gorgeous vessels, "launched on the bosom of the silver Thames," are wafting to distant lands the produce of this commercial nation. Thus all the mercantile glories crowd my fancy, emblazoned in the most refulgent coloring of an ardent imagination. I see sumptuous palaces rising to receive me; I see orphans, and widows, and painters, and poets, and musicians, and builders, protected and encouraged; and when the fabric is pretty nearly finished in my shattered pericranium, I cast my eyes around, and find John Andre, by a small coal fire in Warnford Court; not so tall as he has been making himself, and in all probability, never to be much more than he is at present. But oh! my dear Honora! it is for thy sake only I wish for wealth!"

In the mercantile business he spent a number of years, alternately relieving his mind from the tediousness of his employment, by visiting his friends at Claptan, and his dear Honora at Litchfield. But alas! misfortune had

marked him for her prey. His Utopian castle, which his
"ardent imagination" had reared with such enthusiasm,
vanished from his view; and left him wretched, although
not entirely hopeless. To Honora's father, Maj. Andre
had never been a great favorite, after his attentions to
his daughter; for what reason, is not known; but, probably, because he concluded Andre's turn of mind was illy
calculated for the acquirement of property; at any rate,
after using his influence to dissolve the connection without
success, he exerted his parental authority and accomplished
his purpose, but at the expense of the happiness of his
daughter, and her noble, gallant Andre! Four years
after this event, Honora was induced to marry another
gentleman; but was melancholy and unhappy, and died
of consumption a few months previous to the execution
of Maj. Andre in America.

When the match was thus authoritatively broken off,
Maj. Andre obtained a commission in the British army,
served a while in Germany, and then came to America
early in the revolutionary war. In time, he was appointed
by Sir Henry Clinton Adjutant-General, with the rank of
Major, and became a great favorite with officers and soldiers of the British army.

In 1780 Gen. Arnold had communications with the
British officers for the purpose of surrendering into their
hands West Point, the strongest fortress in America; in
which were deposited supplies for the army, and which
completely guarded the pass of the Hudson river, through
the Highlands. To accomplish this, the British sloop of
war, Vulture, commanded by Capt. Sutherland, came
up the river to Haverstraw Bay, about twenty miles from
West Point, with Col. Beverly Robinson, an American
who adhered to the royal cause, and Maj. Andre. To effect a meeting, Gen. Arnold sent Joshua H. Smith, who
resided near the bay, with a flag of truce to the Vulture

in the night. The object was to effect a meeting on shore
between Maj. Andre and Arnold; but, to blind Smith,
the request was made for Col. Robinson. When Smith
arrived at the Vulture, and delivered his message to Robinson, he excused himself from meeting Arnold on account
of ill health, and introduced to him Maj. Andre, under
the assumed name of Anderson, and said all the purposes
could be effected by his going ashore instead of himself.
The place of interview was at the foot of Long Clove
Mountain, on the Western shore; and on the arrival of
Smith and Maj. Andre, they found Gen. Arnold among
the fir trees. Arnold pretended to be vexed and disappointed at not seeing Col. Robinson; but requested Mr.
Smith to stay with the hands at the boat while he conferred with Mr. Anderson. Smith staid till the dawn of
day, and then thought it prudent to apprise them of it.
Soon after, they both came down to the beach, and Arnold
requested Smith to conduct Mr. Anderson on board the
Vulture. But as the distance was so great, and the
hands fatigued, and as it would be impossible to go and
return before sunrise, he refused. Smith accordingly returned the boat to the place where he had embarked, and
Arnold and Andre, mounted on horseback, rode up to
Smith's house. When Smith arrived at the place to leave
the boat, he observed a cannonading from Gallows Point
against the Vulture, which compelled her to drop down
the river. When he arrived at his own house, he found
that Andre and Arnold had arrived long before, and appeared vexed that the ship had been compelled to leave
her position. After breakfast, Smith retired to recover
from the fatigues of the night, for he was in ill health,
and left Arnold and Andre the greater part of the day
together. Towards evening Arnold came to him and requested that he should convey Mr. Anderson to the Vulture, which had then nearly regained its former position.

But, as Smith had then an ague fit upon him, he was unable to comply. Arnold then requested him to accompany him a part of the way to New York, by land, when his ague fit left him. To this he made no objection. Soon after, Arnold said a difficulty had occurred, of which he was not before apprised: Mr. Anderson had come ashore in military dress, and as it would be impossible for him to travel in that dress, he requested a loan of one of Smith's coats; the other part of his dress required no change. Smith accordingly furnished a coat; and Arnold, having given a pass to Maj. Andre, by the name of John Anderson, to go to White Plains; and Smith, with a flag of truce to go there and return, left them and returned to West Point. Andre appeared disconsolate and sad, and Smith tried to amuse him by showing him from the top of his house the beautiful prospect over the capacious bay and the opposite shore; but he cast an anxious look towards the Vulture, and with a sigh wished himself safely aboard.

At length, Smith, finding himself better, ordered the horses, and they reached the ferry at Stony Point before dark. They called at the Sutlers' and drank with them, then crossed the river and rode on five or six miles, when they were challenged by a patrol party. The commanding officer demanded a countersign, and a reason for their travelling in the night. Smith told him they had passports from Gen. Arnold, which they had that day received; that they were on public business of the utmost importance, and that he would be answerable for their detention a moment. On coming to a light, they presented their passports, and satisfied the officer. He, however, advised them not to proceed in the night, as patroling parties of both armies were out, and there was little chance of avoiding them; and added, he had heard a firing a few minutes before meeting them. Alarmed at

this intelligence, they concluded to go no further that
night, although Andre was anxious to proceed. They returned a short distance and obtained lodgings.

They both slept in the same bed, and Smith was often
disturbed by the restless motions and uneasiness of mind
exhibited by his bed-fellow, who, on observing the first
dawn of day, summoned the servant to prepare the horses
for their departure. They rode cheerfully towards Pine's
bridge, over Croton river, a branch of the Hudson, without interruption ; and as they were passing along, the
countenance of Andre brightened into a cheerful serenity ;
he became affable, and displayed a knowledge in the belles
lettres, music, painting, poetry, and general history, beyond what his companion had any idea he possessed. So
fine was the morning, so pleasant the converse, and so
rich the scenery around them, they became insensible of
time and distance, and were surprised to find themselves
so soon at the bridge ; the contemplated place of their
separation. After breakfasting at a low Dutch house near
the bridge ; and after Smith had given his companion the
necessary directions of his route to the White Plains, on
crossing the bridge ; they took an affecting leave of each
other, and Smith returned to his family in safety.

Andre, on arriving at the fork of the roads, concluded
the one by the White Plains would be circuitous to go to
New York, and having a good horse, he boldly ventured
to take the other down the river. He had proceeded about
six miles, when he was stopped in a narrow part of the
road near Tarrytown, by three New York militia-men,
John Paulding, David Williams, and Isaac Van Vest,
who were on a scouting party between the outposts of the
two armies. One of them having seized his horse by the
bridle, Andre, instead of producing his passport, asked
where they belonged to. They answered, " To below."
Not suspecting deception, he replied, " So do I ;" and

declaring himself a British officer, entreated that he might
not be detained, as he was on pressing business! On
finding himself in the hands of his enemies, he offered
them a valuable gold watch to let him pass; but this led
to further suspicion; they, therefore, took him aside into
the bushes, and searching him, found his papers lodged
in one of his boots! The captors then took him to Col.
Jamison, where he still passed under the name of Anderson; and with a view of providing for the safety of Gen.
Arnold, requested permission to send a line to inform him
of his detention. Astonishing as it may appear, his request was granted. Maj. Andre's messenger arrived at
Gen. Arnold's lodgings, (which were then, at the house
formerly occupied by Col. Robinson, on the opposite side
of the river from West Point, and a short distance from
the shore,) before the messenger Col. Jamison despatched
to Gen. Washington with Andre's papers, and also a letter
from Andre, disclosing his real name and his rank in the
British army, arrived. Gen. Arnold, on the receipt of
the letter, seized the messenger's horse, rode furiously
down a precipice, almost perpendicular, to the river,
jumped into a boat, and ordered the hands to row down
to the Vulture; but he had scarcely passed Verplank's
Point, when Col. Hamilton arrived with orders to stop
him; for about the time Washington reached Robinson's
house, on his return from Hartford, the packet from Col.
Jamison arrived.

Maj. Andre was captured on the 23d of September,
1780; and conducted by a strong guard to Robinson's
house, where he was examined by Gen. Washington; he
was then conducted by water to Stony Point, and by land
to Orange Town, or Tappan. On the 25th of September,
Gen. Washington appointed a board of fourteen general
officers to examine into Maj. Andre's case, and report in
what light he was to be considered, and to what punish-

ment liable. Maj. Andre, before the board of officers, nobly disdaining to shield himself under any evasive subterfuge, and solely anxious to place his character in the fairest point of view, voluntarily declared even more than was required; and palliated nothing in which he himself had been concerned. No witnesses were examined before the board; and after taking time for consideration, they concluded to report, although it is said not unanimously: *" that Maj. John Andre, Adjutant-General of the British army, ought to be considered as a spy from the enemy, and that, agreeably to the law and usage of nations, he ought to suffer death."* After this report of the Court of Inquiry was known, the British officers used every possible exertion that ingenuity could invent, to snatch the gallant Andre from his impending fate; flags of truce were continually passing and repassing between the armies; letters were written in the most masterly manner, calculated to touch the feelings of Gen. Washington; conferences were held between the officers of the opposing armies, &c., &c.; but all, *all* proved unavailing! Andre, understanding that his fate was fixed, and the mode of his death, addressed a letter to Gen. Washington, in which he says: " Let me hope, sir, that if aught in my character impresses you with esteem towards me; if aught in my misfortunes marks me as the victim of policy, and not of resentment, I shall experience the operations of these feelings in your breast, by being informed I am not to die on a *gibbet."* As the mode of his execution was determined on, the feelings of Maj. Andre were spared, by not answering this letter. On the morning of the 2d of October, the unfortunate Andre was led forth to the place of execution. As he passed along, the American army were astonished at the dignity of his deportment; and the manly complacency of countenance which bespoke the serene composure of his mind. The scene was overwhelming; every heart throbbed with anguish, while tears of sensibility flowed from every eye. He bowed to those he had known during his confinement; and coming in view of the fatal spot, and seeing the preparations for his execution, he stopped, as if absorbed in thought; then quickly turning to the officer next him, exclaimed—"What! must I die in this manner?" Being told it was so ordered, he instantly said, "I am reconciled, and submit to my fate, but deplore the mode—it will be but a momentary pang;" and proceeding with calmness, mounted the scaffold, adjusted the fatal cord himself, and requested the surrounding spectators to bear witness to the world, THAT HE DIED LIKE A BRAVE MAN. His body was interred in an open field, near the place of his execution; a consecrated spot, where friends and foes mingle their sorrows, and together deplore the untimely exit of a man possessed of such rare accomplishments, fascinating manners, and nobleness of mind. His name is immortal, not only as being connected with the great events of the revolution, but as it exhibited to the world a character truly amiable and heroic, and universally admired by adversaries and friends.

IN MEMORIAM.

On the second day of October, 1879, Cyrus W. Field erected a shaft at Tappan, N. Y., to mark the spot where Maj. Andre suffered the extreme penalty of the law, Oct. 2d, 1780. It stands in the old orchard on Andre Hill, in Rockland County, near the village of Tappan. The workmen had placed the shaft in position, and it was uncovered at noon, the same hour that Andre was hanged. Not more than twenty persons were present, and not a word was spoken by any one.

The shaft is of Maine granite, and is 3½ feet square and 5 feet in height. It stands on two granite stones as bases, which in turn rest on a heavy stone foundation under ground. There is no ornamentation, the smooth and glistening surface being relieved only by inscriptions in the most modest lettering. On the side toward the West the longest inscription is carved, as follows :

Here died, Oct. 2, 1780, MAJOR JOHN ANDRE, of the British Army; who, on entering the American lines on a secret mission to Benedict Arnold for the surrender of West Point, was taken prisoner, tried and condemned as a spy. His death, though according to the stern code of war, moved even his enemies to pity, and both armies mourned the fate of one so young and so brave. In 1821 his remains were received at Westminster Abbey. One hundred years after his execution, this stone was placed above the spot where he lay, by a citizen of the States against which he fought, not to perpetuate the record of strife, but in token of those better feelings which have since united two nations one in race, in language and in religion, with the earnest hope that this friendly union will never be broken.

Beneath was the name,—

"Arthur Penrhyn Stanley, Dean of Westminster."

On the South side the inscription reads as follows :—

"Sunt Lacrymæ rerum et mentem mortalia tangunt."
—Virgil, Æneid I, 462.

The only other inscription is upon the North side, and is this :—

"He was more unfortunate than criminal ;
An accomplished man, and a gallant officer."
—George Washington.

An inscription will be placed on the East side next year, the centennial of the execution.

This Andre shaft stands on a high elevation, about two and a half miles from the Hudson, and not more than thirty yards from the New Jersey line, overlooking a beautiful country. Mr. Field has bought thirteen acres of land in the immediate vicinity, running to, but not crossing, the New Jersey line. He purposes to convert this property into a park, with two entrances, and carriage-ways leading to a circular drive around the shaft, which will be surrounded by an iron railing. It is stated that when completed he will present the property to the citizens of Tappan. Four trees, two English and two American, either oak or elm, will be planted at the cardinal points around the monument.

Some doubts have been raised as to the exact spot where Andre was buried, but Mr. Field entertains no doubt that he has selected the right place. David D. Brower, John H. Outwater, and John J. Griffith, old residents of Tappan, agree that the spot now marked by the shaft is the exact spot where they saw Andre's remains exhumed in 1821, when the British Government sent the Duke of York to America to convey them to their resting place in Westminster Abbey.

The members of the party from New York were the guests of Mr. Whittemore, and in his company visited the old mansion used by Washington as his headquarters, in the parlor of which he signed Andre's death warrant, the Maby Tavern or " '76 Stone House," in which Andre was confined during his trial and from which he walked to his execution, the site of the church in which Andre was tried, and the camping ground of the hostile armies.

CAPT. NATHAN HALE.

It is said that Mr. Field intends to erect a shaft to the memory of Capt. Nathan Hale of the Continental army, on the spot where he was executed as a spy by the British in 1776. That place is said to be on the public grounds near Hamilton Park, in the city of New York. The execution of Capt. Hale was four years previous to that of Maj. Andre, and the circumstances attending it are in strong contrast with each other; although between the two men there seems to have been a striking resemblance. Both died in the full vigor of early manhood: Hale was aged 21, and Andre 29 years.

Hale was born in Coventry, Ct., on the 6th of June, 1755, and graduated at Yale College with distinction in September, 1773; and like Andre had wooed and won a fair lady at the early age of eighteen. And in person there was a strong resemblance, while in mind, manners and acquirements, they were on a par with each other. After Hale left college, he became a school teacher, and was universally beloved and popular, both with parents and pupils. A lady of his acquaintance said: "Everybody loved him, he was so sprightly, intelligent and kind, and so handsome."

He was teaching school at New London, Ct., when an express arrived bringing tidings of the battles of Lexington and Concord. A town meeting was held, and young Hale was one of the most ardent speakers. He urged an instant march to the scene of hostilities, and offered to enlist himself. He writes to his father: "A sense of duty urges me to sacrifice everything for my country." He went at once, and served as lieutenant in the army before Boston ; and prevailed on his men to extend their enlistment, by giving them his own pay. For his good conduct, he received from Congress a commission as Captain.

He was attached to Col. Knowlton's regiment ; and after the disastrous battle of Long Island, Gen. Washington applied to that officer for a competent person to penetrate the enemy's camp, and learn the condition of the British army. The patriotic Hale promptly volunteered to perform that perilous task, though fully aware of the consequences if captured.

In the character of a school-master, he crossed the Sound from Norwalk to Huntington, on Long Island ; visited the British encampments unsuspected, made drawings of their works, and took notes in Latin. This completed, he turned his steps to Huntington, where a boat from the American shore was to meet him and convey him back to Connecticut. Unfortunately, a British guard ship was anchored round a point out of sight, and had sent a boat ashore for water. It being the time and place of the expected boat, young Hale stepped aboard of the British boat, and found himself a prisoner. He was searched, and his papers were found in the soles of his shoes, which clearly proved him to be a spy. He was taken to the headquarters of General Howe, in New York city, and, after a brief parley with a court martial, was ordered for execution the next morning at daybreak ! He asked for a Bible, but the infamous Cunningham refused the request, and seized and destroyed a letter he had written to his mother ; and said, "The rebels shall never know they have a man who can die with such firmness." But his patriotic spirit shone forth in his dying words—"I only regret that I have but one life to lose for my country."

Now, here are two men, guilty of the same offence according to martial law, and both suffered the same penalty; but how unlike the circumstances attending their execution! Maj. Andre was granted all the privileges compatible with his situation, and died lamented by both armies; Capt. Hale was executed in hot haste, denied all grantable privileges; cursed while living, and execrated when dead! If British officers could take any pleasure in such enormities, no decent man will envy them their feelings.

In the present state of society, wars, more or less, will exist, and efficient, but merciful, generals or commanding officers will be needed; but we may be thankful that some improvement has been made, both in the criminal code and martial law. The ancients crucified criminals, and enslaved, or tortured and put to death prisoners taken in war. Now, criminals are executed without needless pain; and prisoners taken in war are exchanged, or set at liberty on parole, and permitted to return to their own homes again. To prevent wars, strong but just governments are needed. Well it may be asked, why are there no Indian wars in Canada? Simply this,—the strong government there renders it impossible for lawless backwoodsmen to exist. The Indians have rights there which white men are bound to respect. If such power were exerted on this side of the line, there would be no more Indian wars in the United States.

It may sometimes be needful to spy out an enemy's camp, but a commander does not seem justified in inducing any one to enter upon such a perilous undertaking. Better employ balloons, as was done in the last German and French war. But war is a savage operation at best; and as brute force is not argument, and settles nothing, it is time that wars should cease, by the universal consent of all mankind.

FINIS.